An F4
(FRIENDS 4 UPT
PUBLICA....

'Supporting our local library; promoting Creative Writing'

IN PARTNERSHIP WITH THE BEACON PROJECT
and
DORSET COMMUNITY ACTION

ASSISTED BY THE NATIONAL LOTTERY

LADY IN THE RED ANORAK AND OTHER STORIES

AN ANTHOLOGY OF THE ENTRIES TO UPTON LIBRARY'S SHORT STORY COMPETITION 2012

To Catherine

Happy Reading and

Best Wishes from Mike

Adrian Ford, Editor
Jean Tanner, Assistant Editor

Copyright © 2012 *Lady in the Red Anorak and Other Stories* by F4UL Publishing as a compilation.

Copyright © 2012 Individual stories by the authors.

A catalogue record of this book is available from the British Library.

ALL RIGHTS RESERVED under UK and International Copyright conventions. No part of this book may be reproduced, stored in a retrieval system or transmitted in any form, electronic, mechanical, or by other means, without the written permission of the publisher.

This collection of short stories contains works submitted to the Publisher by individual authors who confirm that the work is their original creation. Based upon the authors' confirmations and to the Publisher's actual knowledge, the stories were written by the listed authors. F4UL does not guarantee or assume responsibility for verifying the authorship of each work.

The views expressed within certain stories contained in this anthology do not necessarily reflect the views of the editors or F4UL's committee.

COVER PICTURE: *Barbara Evans*   COVER DESIGN: *CMP (UK) Limited*

PUBLISHED BY F4UL, UPTON LIBRARY, UPTON, DORSET BH16 5PW
'Supporting our local library; promoting Creative Writing'

First published November 2012

First reprint January 2013

Printed in Dorset

By

CMP (uk) Limited
www.cmp-uk.com

CONTENTS

	Page
FOREWORD	8
ACKNOWLEDGEMENTS	10
EDITOR'S NOTE	12
A FEW WORDS FROM THE CHAIRMAN, F4UL	15-16
PRIZEWINNERS	17
SHORT-LIST	18
LIST OF AUTHORS	19-20

SUBMISSIONS TO THE COMPETITION

..................Short List	21-69
..................Alphabetical by Title	71-254
..................Under-18s	255-278
INDEX by TITLE	279-281
MAIL ORDER DETAILS	281

FOREWORD

When it was mooted at a Friends 4 Upton Library (F4UL) committee meeting that a Short Story competition should be organised to help raise funds for the benefit of local library users no-one foresaw how successful the event would be.

Upton, still referred to as 'the village' is now part of Lytchett Minster and Upton Town, and like many satellites of conurbations it suffers from being on the western fringe of Poole in Dorset. The malaise of course is a diminishing identity, and the symptoms are the gradual erosion of services to the larger political and civic entities, to County and Region. In 2011 there was a very real chance that the Upton Library would be closed, but intervention by local politicians and pressure groups including F4UL saved the library on this occasion.

F4UL wanted to put on an event that was different, that had the capacity to raise funds and most importantly, was 'literary'. So was born the idea of a writing competition with two sections, namely Open and Under 18s, inviting original and unpublished stories of about 1000 words. There would be two prizes linked to the amount of entrance money collected.

The final number of entries was fifty-six, many more than optimistically projected. The presentation was made on the 29th March 2012 and over fifty guests attended to hear the short-listed stories read out either by their authors, or a committee member. One of the stories lent itself to be dramatised and an unusual production of a one-act play was presented by the guest speaker, Nick Allen, the founder of Bere Regis' Creative Writing Group, *Dorset Scribblers* (acting as Bob Cratchit) and a F4UL committee member (Mr Scrooge) in an adaptation of Bob Hitching's *The Interview,* with apologies to Charles Dickens, of course.

Following the enjoyable evening, and after many requests it was decided to publish the stories and perhaps make the competition an annual Upton Literary Event. Let's hope we can do that.

We set out to produce a book using as much local expertise as possible. We have achieved that aim in that the whole endeavour, from project design, art-work, editing, marketing, publicising and publishing to printing and distributing a substantial anthology, has been completed in Dorset. Most of it has been accomplished in Upton.

So here we are: An anthology of the entries to the competition...We hope you find them entertaining and thought-provoking – and a spur, if one is needed, to put digit to keyboard, write an original story and submit it to one of the many and various competitions and publishers.

Adrian Ford
Editor and F4UL Committee Member
Upton, September 2012

ACKNOWLEDGEMENTS

My thanks go to the whole F4UL Committee who helped to get the project going and bring it to fruition. Additionally, I would like to thank Jean Tanner, F4UL Secretary, who assisted with the editing of the Anthology. All committee members and their spouses contributed to making the presentation event a success. Peter Tanner and Kathryn Rusling put in invaluable work in providing the refreshments with Nia Nebel, F4UL Treasurer, and Jean Tanner; Peter was particularly helpful too, with the setting up of the auditorium. Peter Rusling, F4UL Vice-chairman, organised the box-office.

Thanks go to Fiona Tait and those short-listed authors who were present and who delighted the audience with their readings.

My thanks also go to Françoise Griffin, now of The Beacon Project, and PULM for providing the PA system, without which we may well have had a problem. Special thanks go to Ron and Jill Burns for their help in setting up the PA equipment, and also to Nia Nebel for providing the spotlights for the 'play'.

We were indebted to our guest speaker, Nick Allen, the founder of *Dorset Scribblers*, a local Creative Writing Group, who entertained us with a witty and informative speech 'In Praise of the Short Stories', the evening's theme.

We acknowledge and thank DCC and the staff of Upton Library for the use of their facilities.

Thanks go to all the authors and the audience, without whom the Anthology would not have been considered.

A special thank you goes to our venerable Chairman, Fred Drane for his oratory skills in introducing the event and our special guest, and for drawing the evening to a close.

I acknowledge the assistance given to me, a rooky editor, in respect of 'putting the book to bed' by Paul Dawe, Director CMPUK, The Fulcrum, Poole, Dorset and for the finished cover design, to Richard Johnson, Production Manager, CMPUK; and also to the Managing Editor of *Every Day Fiction*, Camille Gooderham Campbell, for waiving their first option to publish *The Ferryman's Wife* in an anthology.

Our thanks also go to Barbara Evans, 'our local illustrator' as she is affectionately known in Upton, for giving her outstanding painting that illustrates so sensitively the essence of the story that gives our anthology its title. The striking artistry of the cover's artwork embellishes our book markedly.

The F4UL committee would like to thank The Beacon Project and their partner, Dorset Community Action and The Big Lottery Fund for their generous donation towards the publication and printing costs of this volume.

Finally, the most important acknowledgement of all goes to you, the purchasers of the Anthology. The profits from the combined sales of the anthology will go to F4UL funds and thence to equipment and the like – our part in making the library increasingly useful and popular to all residents in the local area.

Adrian Ford
F4UL, Committee Member and Editor

EDITOR'S NOTE

One day I saw a lion.
The bad lion was eating a mouse.
A good lion saved the mouse.
The Mouse ran away.

'*Lions*' by Scarlett Cromwell, age 3

Not long after the competition opened I received a submission from a group of mainly younger children under the guidance of Jan Cooke. As it was produced by a group and presented as a booklet none of the stories was part of the competition. However, on reading *Lions* by Scarlett Cromwell I just knew the event would be a success. For one so young to produce what is the essence of the short-story genre – not a word wasted, a beginning, middle and an end, all in twenty-three words, is quite remarkable. Well done, indeed, Miss Cromwell.

Despite circularising many schools the number of entries to the under-18s section was disappointing, but the quality was very high. Subject matter was mainly SF/Fantasy but with vastly different themes from one with echoes of *Toy Story* to the trials and tribulations of a fairy that could not fly, and from a variation on a well-loved children's story to a breathless and full-blown SF thriller. The non-SF story was contemporary, a child's perspective on a particular consequence of a broken marriage. The winner was unanimously chosen: Eloise Orchard's *There's a Wolf in our Oven*. For a ten-year old to produce a well-thought out and original take on a theme that has almost been worked to death, from Disney to Hannah-Barbera to Tel Hachette, is amazing. The plot is not uncomplicated but the author knows where she is taking the reader and does so with panache – and ultimately with humour and a play on words reminiscent of many music-hall greats. A wonderful story, Eloise.
I must also give an honourable mention to Tara Prince's *Life or Death?* a classic, pacey Fantasy short that is not only a very well-constructed tale but also a marvellous read. Well done, Tara.

There were fifty-one entries to the Open section, as a group demonstrating the breadth of imagination and applied skills the judges were hoping for. They were seeking well-constructed tales, written in good English and that lifted the spirit or made us think or cry or made us say, 'That's clever' or 'I did not expect that to happen' and yet be believable. We hoped the stories would be three-dimensional, demonstrating an understanding and use of metaphors and other literary devices, variations in pace where characters would be developed or descriptive phrases used to give depth to the narrative. Most of the criteria were in evidence as many stories were first class efforts, which of course made the judges' task more difficult.

Content varied from an allegorical budgerigar and other birds on the wing to Peeping-Tom building workers with a canny gaffer, from shopping nightmares to an ecclesiastical would-be detective, from teenage angst to a very local love affair and to an elderly lady's poignant and enduring knick-knacks and associated memories. The humorous pieces raised many a smile, all being excellent endeavours in a difficult genre.

The judges whittled the entries down to a short-list of ten. To those forty-one that did not get that far please remember that judges' decisions inevitably are partly subjective and many were very good stories of which the authors should be proud. I particularly enjoyed *Lady in the Red Anorak*, *Messing About on the River* and *The Bag of Memories*.

The short-list comprised ten highly commendable stories including two haunting tales - *The Blue Eyed Boy* and *The Hill Top* and the ingenious *The Interview* performed on the presentation evening as a one-act play as mentioned in the *Foreword above*. *Forever Autumn* is a cleverly constructed extended metaphor in the guise of a memoir of a caged bird. *Not One of Us* is a complete murder mystery in less than one thousand words – quite remarkable; *Love Songs in Blue Denim* is a classic Romance but *Never Ending Love Story* is not what it seems –

much more a mystery unfolding on the Jurassic coast. *My Holiday* makes a relationship between an amnesiac and his psychiatrist, as seen from the patient's perspective, seem light and almost amusing. Between the lines, however, one reads there is much more in this poignant tale.

Our runner-up is a serious story of two troubled people meeting for the first time on a tenement doorstep early one crisp winter's morning in Edinburgh. Sharon Jones's *Whisky Angel* is set in beautiful surroundings but, in sublime juxtaposition, the subject matter is far from benign. Alcoholism and depression combine in a deadly cocktail of despair for the couple in this strong and masterly story.

Whilst it was very difficult to select only ten stories for the short-list, the winner was chosen unanimously. For ingeniousness of plot, skilfully under-played presentation of characters and scene leading to increasing tension and apparent inevitability of conclusion, the author's ability to maintain suspense to the very last sentence, when a cunning resolution that would surprise and delight the most analytical of reader, is awesome. **Richard Nicholson's** *The Ferryman's Wife* **is the very worthy winner of the Upton Library Short Story Competition 2012.**

I enjoyed the reading and assessment of all the submissions immensely. The response was very encouraging and indicative of the huge number of aspiring authors in our local area. I hope our experience this year will help to inspire further literary activity.

Thank you all for your efforts...let's see what comes up next time!

Adrian Ford
Upton, 2012

A FEW WORDS FROM THE CHAIRMAN OF THE FRIENDS 4 UPTON LIBRARY (F4UL)

The Friends 4 Upton Library and their Committee are working hard towards maintaining a local Library fit for purpose. We believe a Library is not only for providing lending facilities for books and DVDs, though that is its prime purpose. We believe the Library should encompass all ages providing many of myriad activities related to the art of reading and writing.

Upton Library welcomes people in to choose from many informative sources in their various forms including large print and audio books. You can read the newspapers, use computers and ask for information. The Library staff and F4UL actively encourage young children to read, and they provide ideas and projects for them. Come and see what is on offer in our Library.

The Friends 4 Upton Library Committee host monthly Talks, Quizzes, Art Competitions and many other activities associated with an active and community-driven support to a threatened Library service. We shall pursue our aims as long as the public wants us to – and gives *us* support in our turn.

We raise as much money as we can in order to improve the Library by supplying, for example, additional equipment that helps the Library to provide the level of service required to keep it viable - and open. But, we need more!

Our latest project was a Short Story Competition, open to all ages. It grabbed the imagination of nearly forty authors around the local area, from ages three to over seventy-nine. Following the presentation evening that was enjoyed by so many, I was asked on numerous occasions 'what happens next?' And after a bit of lateral thinking the idea took seed and now this wonderful

Anthology has come to fruition. I hope you read the book, and enjoy.

Please help us in our endeavours by joining us by becoming a Friend 4 Upton Library. An application form is provided with this book; there are more at the Library.

Thank you.

**Cllr. Fred Drane (Town, Purbeck and County)
Chairman, F4UL**

PRIZE WINNERS 2012

OPEN SECTION:

RICHARD NICHOLSON

'THE FERRYMAN'S WIFE'

UNDER 18s SECTION:

ELOISE ORCHARD

'THERE'S A WOLF IN OUR OVEN'

SHORT LIST

Forever Autumn	Caroline	Hall
Love Songs in Blue Denim	Della	Millward
My Holiday	Keith	Hart
Never Ending Love Story	Mike	Lawrence
Not One of Us	Janice	Kirkby-Brown
The Blue Eyed Boy	Jo	Maycock
The Ferryman's Wife	Richard	Nicholson
The Hill Top	Jackie	Macintosh
The Interview	Bob	Hitching
Whisky Angel	Sharon	Jones

LIST OF AUTHORS

PAGE/S

Bossons	Lydia	261
Brown	Hannah	265
Burnett-Thomas	Irene	231
Chambers	George	85
Connolly	Clare	205
Coward	Mary	227
Eastwood	Olive	165
Grant	Jenny	137
Hall	Caroline	27
Hart	Keith	33
Haway	Moira	189
Hitching	Bob	59,77,97,149,237,241,251
Hitching	Licia	153
Holman	Diana	133
Hughes	Ruth	221
Jones	Sharon	65
Kirkby	Charles	81
Kirkby-Brown	Janice	45,145
Lawrence	Mike	39,71,125,169,185
Macintosh	Jackie	55
Maley	Tim	159
Maycock	Jo	51
Millward	Della	31,211
Morris	Valerie	91
Naish	Tim	107
Nicholson	Richard	21

Nourse	Janette	129
O'Grady	Shelagh	195
Orchard	Eloise	256
Perkins	Janette	155
Petersen	Anne	101
Piercy	Jenny	245
Prince	Tara	269
Sams	Daniel	199
Saunders	Clive	181
Scally	S J	119,217
Sharp	Kathy	113
Taylor	Rebekah	273

THE FERRYMAN'S WIFE

Richard Nicholson

(First published on-line in *Every Day Fiction*, August 2012)

On a still November night the water in the creek slipped silently past the village, unseen by black windowed houses. Two jetties stretched out as if the village was dipping its fingers into the inky water. A low cry from a tar-black clapperboard house broke the stillness as Widow Jonas slept fitfully, yearning for her long-dead husband from her bed of camphor and worn cotton. In a similar house at the end of the other jetty a light burned in the window. Tom Dewey, the ferryman, sat and stared out across the creek. His wife was coughing in her troubled sleep in the back room. Her fever had burned for three days and nights and showed no sign of abating.

Suddenly a light pierced the darkness from the far bank and waved back and forth to attract the ferryman's attention. Tom lifted his lantern and signalled in recognition, then crept into the adjoining room. His wife's skin was hot to the touch as he removed the cloth from her brow, rinsed it in the bowl on the washstand and replaced it. He leaned over and kissed the top of her greying head and quietly closed the door behind him. In the porch he put on a shapeless woollen coat and a pair of sea boots, the stiff oiled leather protesting as he pulled them on, and walked with unhurried steps down the track to the jetty where his boat was moored.

Tom rowed with the steady strokes of a man who earns his living on the water and with customers who can't go anywhere else in a hurry. He glanced over his shoulder now and again to get his bearings against the current as he neared the tall cloaked figure waiting for passage. The salty odour of the mudflats cut through the low mist that hung will o' the wisp on the water so even Tom, twenty years on the creek, could smell it at low tides like this. He brought the boat alongside the jetty, threw a rope around a post and turned to look at his passenger standing above him, hooded against the chill of the night.

'Passage is two pennies,' said Tom.

'I'll pay one penny now and the other when we get to the other side,' said the man. Tom nodded and held the boat steady while the passenger stepped in, made himself comfortable on a bench in the stern and handed Tom a penny. He felt a brief spark of energy pass between them at the moment they both touched the coin, but the passenger seemed not to notice. Tom cast off and bending against the oars, turned the sharp prow of the boat into the current before heading off across the creek.

'What is your business to be out so late on a night like this?' he asked his passenger.

'I am Death,' said his passenger, 'and I have come to collect the soul of your wife.'

Tom Dewey missed his stroke, his starboard oar found air not water, and he struggled to keep his seat as Death stretched out a skeletal hand to grip the side of the rocking boat.

'Be careful,' said Death, in a calm voice. 'You know you can't swim and I've no call on your soul just yet.' Tom felt as if the chill river mist had entered his heart. His breathing became shallow and cold sweat ran down his neck soaking his collar.

'But my wife is not dead,' he said. 'I left her sleeping.'

'She has the fever,' said Death, 'and she will be dead by the time I arrive.'

Tom regained his balance and dipped both oars into the gloomy water. He took a stroke, then paused and leaned forward on the oars raising them above the surface so that diamonds of water dripped softly creating a myriad of circles on the creek.

'It's no good,' said Death, as if reading his thoughts. 'You can't kill Death. There is nothing you can do to prevent it from happening.'

Tom's clothes were soaked with fear. The crushing futility of his existence suddenly crowded in on him. He shook with silent grief.

'Will you be gentle with her? Will it hurt?'

'She won't feel a thing from me,' said Death. 'I will arrive at the final breath.'

Tom glanced over his shoulder and through his tears picked out the jetty and headed towards it. As he drew alongside he shipped both oars and glided beside the rotting piles, slowing the boat until it stopped. Death stretched out his hand offering the other penny.

'I'll not take money for my wife,' Tom said. He tied up and held the boat steady, tears streaming down his face.

'She's in the back room,' Tom sobbed as Death strode purposefully towards the house without a backwards glance.

Tom fell back into the bottom of the boat, his arms hugging his knees in a cocoon of grief, rocking backwards and forwards in silent screaming anguish.

'What have I done?' he asked himself over and over.

Presently he stood up stiffly, climbed onto the jetty and walked up to his house. He took his boots off in the porch and silently entered the front room. All was still. He lit a candle and carried it towards the door of the bedroom, his stockinged feet wet on the dusty floor-boards. His wife lay on the bed, her thin form lifeless under the covers. Tom sat on the bed and took her cool hand in his.

'The fever has broken,' his wife whispered, her fingers fluttering in his grasp. She turned her head to look at him with her pale blue eyes. Tom nodded, lifted her hand to his lips and kissed it.

'Get some rest now,' he said. 'I'll sleep on the chair.' He stood up. 'Widow Jonas was taken from us tonight. I'm just going to move the boat up to our jetty and I'll be back in.'

FOREVER AUTUMN

Caroline Hall

Few of us appreciate the sweet solace of ignorance; but when it is gloriously and brutally snatched away, the pain can be almost too much to bear.

Fortunately for Tamar, the blessings bestowed upon the seagulls, free to scatter the seashore on a falling tide, can never even be imagined by a budgerigar. Tamar had only ever known the bars of a cage and he was content in the knowledge that although the mighty phoenix of the heavens had made his kind exotic in their beauty; yet their inheritance was to a life of captivity.

Tamar's cage was positioned inside a bigger enclosure, where birds with no wings attended him. They brought him food and water and pieces of cuttlefish for his beak, and also saw to it that his cage was kept free from mess and debris. These birds with no wings were kind to him and served him well, but they did not stir him from his apathy. There was one source of fascination for Tamar and this was a large panel of light which dominated the end of the enclosure. He felt sure that the mighty winged phoenix of the heavens had more in store for his feathered creatures than these bars of solitude.

Today, Tamar knew that he was to be swept clean. He recognised the packets of scratchy sheets that were to line the bottom of his cage. Unusually however, it was the *small* bird with no wings who was attending to him. She had never taken on this job before and it seemed to take her a long time. The cage was left clean enough and she looked pleased with herself. That was until she clumsily knocked the piece of cuttlefish which jammed the bars, to the floor of the cage. She opened up a hole in the bars to retrieve it and ran off. Tamar had never known his cage to be open before and his little heart began to stir and flutter in anticipation. He took off from his perch without hesitation. The confines of his cage had meant that he had never even tried to stretch his wings before and whether they would carry him or not, he had no idea. He flew towards the panel of light and to his amazement this also became another opening to a greater, more marvellous world. The

28

colours were vibrant and he seemed to breathe life itself from the very breath of the mighty phoenix. A feeling of elation fizzled through his body but he felt himself tire and his wings became heavy through lack of use. He landed heavily and then instantly felt pinned down by things that scratched him. He relaxed for a moment and it was at this point that he realised that his struggles had not gone unnoticed. Another small bird stood, just a claws length away from him. Tamar noticed how plain he looked, apart from a little rosy puff on his belly.

'You're in a fix now,' trilled the robin. 'The garden is no place for your kind. You wouldn't last one winter and if you stay in that bush; the hawk will get you. You must return back to where you came from, before it is too late.'

Tamar had no intention of returning. A little piece of ignorance had been chipped away, revealing new hopes that a budgerigar would never normally have dreamt of. Then, suddenly, he felt himself being picked up by the small bird with no wings, which had sought and found him and gleefully she put him back in his cage.

Time passed slowly for Tamar. He searched constantly for the hole and pushed himself against the bars in vain. He began to stretch his wings and practised flapping them each day. Next time he would not fall. Next time they would carry him on.

There was much activity in the enclosure today. Birds with no wings were rushing around purposefully, until finally he felt his cage being picked up and he was taken somewhere new. This enclosure was quite wonderful to Tamar. Each side was a panel of light, through which he could see a garden, just like the one where the bird with the rose - puff belly lived. Then something else caught his eye. Another bird, like him, with feathers yellow and brilliant flew down to him. She perched on the hole to his cage and together they flew; together they twittered their melodies to the mighty winged phoenix of the heavens and Tamar felt his little heart quiver. The richness of his feathers, sapphire blue reflected the riches that he felt inside. As their beaks caressed, he felt another piece of ignorance chip away and the dull monotony of his past existence disappeared. Each day dawned with the wonder of new discoveries to be made.

One day they were sleeping on the perch inside his cage, when she was suddenly taken from him and the hole in his cage was closed. He was then carried back to another, darker enclosure which he recognised. A cobweb now hung in the corner and he was placed in a familiar position, facing the panel of light. The cushion of ignorance had been removed and his little heart lay exposed to the taunts of despair which wage war when hopes have been dashed.

White fluffy flakes now fringed the panel of light with the intricacies of an Egyptian fresco. Through this screen, Tamar fancied that he saw his friend with the rose – puff belly. He appeared cold and hungry, yet his eyes conveyed pity and regret for the creature with the beautiful sapphire feathers, who had felt the breath of the mighty phoenix in his wings and the warmth of his golden companion at his side. The Indian summer of opportunity had faded and blown away in the autumn breeze and for Tamar, there was no return.

LOVE SONGS IN BLUE DENIM

Della Millward

Editor's Note:

It is with great regret that we are unable to print Della Millward's story as the serial rights and first option to print have been sold to a national magazine. We, of course, congratulate Della on her success and look forward to its publication.

Luckily she entered two into the competition. *'The Domino Effect'* can be found on page 211.

AF

MY HOLIDAY

Keith Hart

Mr Cave, my psychiatrist, is once more saying that it's important to remember who I am because the people who love me are very distressed about my condition. I tell him, again, that they shouldn't worry because I am very happy right now, even if I don't know why.

'It's like being on a really good holiday. I think whoever I am didn't take many holidays and I'm enjoying the change of scenery.'

'Tell me more Kenneth. What's this holiday like?'

'It must be one of those all-inclusive holidays with food and drink whenever you need it, as long as you don't mind tea and coffee instead of wine or whisky. There's plenty of time for reading, and thinking, and no-one asks you for anything. I have a room on the ground floor with a big picture window, and my own bathroom. There are no reports to write, no people to see, and my time is my own, except when I come to see you, of course. I have no responsibilities. It's nice being me for a change.'

Mr Cave writes in his notebook, puts down the pen, removes his spectacles and gives me his amused look, the one that makes me feel like a wayward child.

'I think you must have been very tired before your accident Kenneth.'

I do not reply because I know what comes next. I say I don't know what he means, then he'll try to force me to remember, then I'll start to cry, and he will say goodbye till the next time we meet.

'You see Kenneth, you were tired and stressed before the accident. You are an important person with lots of responsibility. There are people waiting for you to get better. Some of them can't have a holiday until you've finished yours. That's not very fair, is it?'

'No, I suppose not.'

I hang my head and feel a tear building in my eye. I stare down, trying not to blink because when I do it will drip on the carpet and he will see that I am crying.

Mr Cave ignores me, like he always does when he's about to make one of his speeches.

'You've had a frightening experience, not to mention a bump on the head, and your mind has put a strategy in place to avoid thinking about it, because it's painful. It's persuaded you that you can escape reality by building a construct that you are in a place you always wanted to go. It's a sanctuary, a world away from real life, where nothing bad happens. This holiday of yours is a fantasy Kenneth. Until you let it go you will never remember who you are.'

I stare into the distance and refuse to listen any more. I like this holiday. I feel safe. I have no expectations. I never feel disappointed. Most of all, I do not have to remember anything. Without memories I can just be myself.

When I first met Mr Cave, when he still called me Mr Sinclair, I had some memories that wouldn't go away. I could remember a close up view of Tottenham High Road. It was as if I had been doing press-ups on the pavement and several people were standing on me, pressing my face into the concrete slabs. I pushed into my hands to raise myself up but I lacked the strength. I saw the horse above me and the horseshoe coming down in slow motion. I remember admiring the surprising symmetry and beauty in the underside of a horse's foot. Why had I never seen this before? I blinked. The next thing I saw was the face of Mr Cave.

This memory triggers another and I start talking.

'Last night I remembered something. I was watching a mob throwing bricks through shop windows. I was shouting instructions to people wearing uniforms. They did what I told them and it felt good. Then I was standing in front of a row of microphones and people were asking me questions but they never listened to the answers. They just kept asking more questions. That made me angry inside. Then I woke up.'

I stop talking. I did not mean to reveal any of this because I know Mr Cave will want more, and I have no more to give.

Mr Cave scribbles in his book and nods at the clock on the wall behind me.

'That's excellent Kenneth. We can work on this in tomorrow's session. Why don't you go back to that memory and focus on the uniforms? What colour are they? Do you like them? Have you ever worn a uniform like it? How does it make you feel? The answers to these questions could be the key that opens the portal into your real world, the real you. Tomorrow could be an exciting day!'

'Goodbye, Mr Cave.' I shake his hand, leave the room and follow the nurse back to my room. As we pass through a reception area I pick up the evening paper. Inside my room I spend the next hour reading every word of every article, paying particular attention to the photographs, with my scissors and my scrapbook ready but once more, there is nothing worth saving.

I open the scrapbook and look at the first page, the only page that isn't blank, and read out the caption below the photograph.

"Assistant Commissioner Kenneth Sinclair was seriously injured on the first night of the riots."

I have a strong urge to take this to Mr Cave. I should tell him this is the picture of a man who deserves a holiday but I know he is incapable of appreciating the refuge I have found. Although he is an intelligent man he would not recognise my oasis. In his hands my desert island would become a mirage. He would not listen. He would not understand. Mr Cave doesn't understand holidays.

NEVER ENDING LOVE STORY

Mike Lawrence

Frank Holden, the Coroner's officer, pawed through the bagged contents of the man's pockets. Standing in the office at the town's mortuary, he quickly established the body's identity. His credit and discount cards, two ten pound notes and most helpful of all, his bus pass, were all readable in the water logged wallet. 'George Falconer.'

The elderly man had been washed up on Boscombe beach. Paramedics and police on the scene found no signs of life, took him to the local A & E and then to the morgue.

Frank went to speak to the village police officer in Studland further down the coast.

'Did you know George Falconer who lived in the retirement flats here?'

'Oh, yes, I often saw him cycling around the area. I had begun to wonder why I hadn't seen him for a couple of days. But now this. Well, I never.' He shook his head. 'Still that might explain the bike.'

'The bike?'

'Yes, he was always on it, every day. About three days ago a chap walking his dogs the other side of Old Harry Rocks reported seeing a bike at the bottom of the cliffs. No sign of anyone, just a bike. I had a look but decided it was too risky to recover it, so I simply logged the find and waited for someone to report it missing.' He agreed it did look like the same type George owned.

The officer tapped the ordnance survey map on the wall indicating the bike's location.

'It's a six hundred feet drop from the highest point,' he claimed, buttoning up his tunic and seeking to make a good impression on one of the Coroner's staff. Nothing much happened in this part of the Purbecks in winter, but now he could be at the heart of a big investigation. 'Could it have been suicide? George would know the downs like the back of his hand; it's unlikely he fell over by accident on or off his bike. You don't think he was mugged, do you?'

Later that morning Frank interviewed the House Manager where George had lived. He had been reported missing three days previously. She told him that George was recently widowed, had neither children nor any listed relatives.

'What happened?' She was eager to learn. 'Was it an accident on his bike?'

Frank left the Manager still none the wiser, returning to his office to read a copy of the Pathologist's report again. "Substantial head injuries...multiple fractures of two limbs...no sea water in either lung indicating death had preceded entry into water and therefore death was not from drowning...the injuries consistent with a fall from height...no evidence of trauma other than striking a solid object such as a rock...One factor yet unexplained; the presence of fine grit under both eyelids and at the back of the eyes." The expert's report was not conclusive because samples of the grit had been sent to the Home Office Pathologist in London which would mean a considerable delay.

He would have to examine George's flat, but a search simply revealed normal paperwork, a modest but sufficient bank balance according to current statements, but no sign of a suicide note. That ruled out that theory. Could he have been pushed by someone or did he cycle too fast and go over the cliff? The weather that morning was fine and George knew the path well. It's going to be put down to death by accident or an open verdict. He could do no more; collect the evidence and present it to the Coroner.

End of story? Not quite.

Had Frank asked the house manager more questions she would have told him that Mr and Mrs Falconer didn't enjoy a happy partnership. In fact, they detested each other. There were constant noisy arguments. He went out on his bike or to the pub each day. He wanted to watch sport on television, but wasn't allowed to. Loved the outdoors, cycling and walking the coast path.

Mary, his wife, had become agoraphobic. Never seen outside the flat. Became addicted to singing and dancing contests on television but hated sport with a vengeance. The couple had grown incompatible.

There was something else that the Coroner's Officer didn't find out. After her death from a heart attack a few months ago, George took to keeping Mary's ashes in an urn in front of the television screen whilst he watched all the sport he could tune into; even subscribing to satellite channels to get more. He also took the urn with him on cycle rides and walks because she hated going out. Was there ever a more hateful relationship?

In a final feat of aggression he decided to take her ashes to the end of the headland at Ballard Down and scatter them to the four winds. Let her be in the open, let her end her days on the coast path!

The last act of spite was going well. George cycled along the path as fast as he could, close to the cliff's edge, holding the topless urn in one hand. He sprinkled the grey grit and laughed as it sprayed along the path.

'That'll teach her,' he shouted. 'How about this, Luv, for a breath of fresh air?'

It seemed the strong gust of wind had come out of nowhere; it was an unusually still day. An up-draught of air blew the ashes back towards unsuspecting George. Suddenly the grey mist-like cloud was in his eyes. Stinging, blinding, painful; he blinked, but couldn't see at all. Over the cliff went George and his bike.

End of the story? Not quite.

Of course we will never know the true ending, not yet anyway. It seemed that Mary, all her problems lifted from her troubled mind, wanted to be with her beloved George once more. There was only one way for him to join her.

End of story? Who knows?

NOT ONE OF US

Janice Kirkby-Brown

Detective Inspector Jack Jones sucked on his peppermint and listened intently while allowing his gaze to wander over the scene, except the area where the body lay. The coroner spoke in terse, half-sentences.

'Okay. Dead about four to six hours. Looks like fell off his bike. But... He was moved. Cause of death - inconsistent. He was hit.'

'You mean by a car?' Jones asked dubiously. He hadn't examined the actual body closely, but the general impression of the scene made a traffic accident seem unlikely. But then, if the body was moved, this may not be the *right* scene.

'No. On the head. Long blunt instrument.' The man started to walk away then shouted over his shoulder. 'Crowbar. Wrench, maybe. Report when I'm done.'

Jones moved across the hotel entrance to where the young receptionist who had found the body and called 999, was standing alongside a police officer.

'So, was the dead guy staying here? A guest maybe? I assume you'd know who he was if he were a member of staff?'

She burst into tears. Oh great. If there was one thing he couldn't deal with at a crime scene it was weeping witnesses. And the bodies, of course. He never was much good at those either.

To the officer he quietly suggested, 'Get one of her mates out here will you, to help calm her down. I need her to start making sense and soon.'

Jones knew if she had anything useful to say he needed to get it from her asap. The longer it took for her to talk about what she'd seen, the more likely it was her mind would start editing the information. It can be the little oddities, the absurdities of a situation that give a killer away. Trouble is, if you think about it, the mind can start playing tricks, saying you *couldn't* have seen something just because it *shouldn't* have been there.

Ten minutes later after a lot of sobbing, nodding and shaking of her head, and with the encouragement of the hotel housekeeper, Jones had learned everything the receptionist new. Nothing. The dead guy wasn't a guest, wasn't staff and she'd seen nobody else and seemingly nothing out of place – except the body draped over his fallen bicycle. He did learn one thing of use though. Somebody in the hotel had to know him. Both the receptionist and the housekeeper confirmed there was no regular path or footpath crossing the grounds, and no exit in the hedged boundary large enough to accommodate a man with a bike, whether he was riding it or not. So why else would a cyclist be on the drive of such a secluded hotel? Unless he was moved up here from the main road...

'Hi Officer. Can I help?'

Jones looked round to see a thick-set, forty-something man with short, slightly greying hair and a distinct air of officious superiority. With him was a petite, rather pretty woman of about the same age. His wife probably, judging from the way she was trying to shush him and pull him back into the hotel.

'What do you think you might be able to do?' he asked, trying not to let the instant dislike he'd felt for the man, show.

'Well, I don't know. If I look at the body, maybe I'd recognise him – or maybe I'd see something you haven't. You know what they say, "Two sets of eyes are better than one". You see, I'm on the job as well, or near as.'

'Brian!'

Jones felt her exasperation as the woman threw up her hands and turned away from her husband, and saw the shock register on her face as she encountered the crime scene for the first time.

'Go back inside. Now.' The man spoke harshly and shoved her toward the hotel entrance. 'This is police business. We don't need hysterical women interfering in our investigation.'

Brian blocked her view, and shoved her again, handling her so roughly she nearly fell.

'That's enough. This is *my* investigation, and I will decide who I talk to and when. And right now I want to talk to your wife.'

'You can't. She doesn't know anything and has nothing to say to you,' the man snarled.

Speaking very gently Jones replied.

'This is what will happen. You will go with this officer,' raising his eyebrows got the officer's attention, 'and sit in that police car. We know the dead man visited someone at this hotel last evening, so my sergeant,' a quick glance to which the sergeant responded, 'is going to check all guests rooms and their cars – and he's going to start with yours while I have a chat with your wife.'

They went to sit in the reception area. Within minutes she had told this gentle, mild-mannered policeman what little she knew. The man's clothing, the bike, looked exactly like Tom's. Brian, was an amateur rally-driver, and Tom his navigator. There was a big race on next week, but this weekend was their anniversary. Neither of them expected Tom to turn up but he had last night, to tell Brian he'd got himself a drive of his own, starting next race. They'd had a big row, but Tom was fine when he left as far as she knew. But Brian was really angry so went to the bar while she went to bed. The sergeant interrupted them.

'You were right boss.'

His gloved hands held an evidence bag – stained clothing and a crowbar from Brian's car. Jones sighed heavily. He should be grateful that so many killers returned to the scene of their crime -and felt the urge to be "helpful" to the police. A thought struck him,

'Ma'am, your husband said he was on the job as well. What does he do, when he's not rally-driving?'

'He's a Traffic Warden,' she said with contempt in her voice.

Jones gave a short, joyless laugh. Yes, of course he was.

THE BLUE EYED BOY

Jo Maycock

The boy was small. As he stood in line with all the other seven year olds he was a good head shorter. She noticed him straight away. He was so still. The other boys shuffled and fidgeted as they tried to stay in line, one boy wandered off and left the room.

She walked, with Bill, along the line, needing to choose. As they came level with the boy he raised his eyes and looked directly at her.

His eyes were *blue*.

In a line of brown skinned children he had blue eyes, a deep, deep blue. He kept his gaze steady, he was perfectly composed in his stillness.

Impulsively, she put out her hand to him and said, 'Would you like to come and live with us?'

She felt rather than saw Bill stiffen and heard his intake of breath.

'Yes please, thank you,' said the boy without a moment's hesitation, as if this was exactly what he expected. Everyone was silent, even the restless boys.

Her husband muttered, 'Steady on, shouldn't we discuss this?'

She turned to him, smiled and then taking the boy's hand, turned back, walked to the door and out into the heat of the day.

At home she showed him the room that was to be his. The bedcover was a cheerful red and white, there was a collection of toy animals on the chest of drawers. The boy seemed pleased, he sat on the bed smiling and looked perfectly at ease.

He was a lovely child, quietly obedient, eager to please. He loved being outside and spent much of his time gazing over the wall into the forest beyond. He spoke very little, she found his presence comforting.

She loved to see him, to be near him. Every morning he would sit on her knee and she would kiss the top of his head and stroke is black shiny curls. She tried to teach him his letters and numbers but his blue eyes would darken and become distant. She did not persist.

One morning, waking later than usual, she hurried downstairs, calling his name. There was no response. She ran from room to room calling the servants. Panic gripped her, it was all happening again. She was bad, wicked, careless, unworthy. Rushing into the garden she found her way to the tree that the pram had been under, on that awful day.

And then she saw him climbing over the back wall.

'Where have you been?' she screamed, tear-stained and distraught.

He looked puzzled for a moment and then spoke in his clear piping voice, 'To visit my people.'

She gathered him to her; he offered no resistance and wound his arms around her neck. They went inside. She tried to get him to explain but he just smiled, nodded and gently patted her face.

She felt it was time to be firm, she made him promise never to scare her like that again, warned of the terrible dangers that lay beyond the wall, the bad people, the wild animals, the rabid dogs. He listened very carefully looking at her face all the time with his huge blue eyes.
As usual, that summer the women and children escaped into the hills in search of cooler air. Every day they gathered at the club house. The children played and swam and their mothers gossiped, sunbathed and complained about the laziness of their servants.

The boy learned to swim. He became like a fish. Soon he had mastered the diving board, entering the water as coolly and calmly as he lived his days. She loved to watch him, her connection to him grew, it became so strong that often they would look around and meet each other's eyes. They would both be amused and smile. Sometimes he would nod, just a little, as if he knew everything about her. This was nonsense, of course. After all, he was a child.

One morning the boy was sitting on her bed amusing himself with some beads. She was dressing, he was singing softly. He stopped his play, seemed to be listening, before climbing down from the bed, looked steadily at her, placing his head against her stomach, and left the room. He was smiling.

It was soon after that the sickness began and she realised she was pregnant. At first she told only the boy; he nodded quite unsurprised. She spoke of her love for him, reassuring him that nothing would change.

Back home things went on much as usual. She grew large and the boy would place his hands over her belly and feel the kicking, dancing baby.

He still spent much of his time outside, alone, walking around the forbidden walls. He sang or hummed. It was a very happy time.

Labour came early. It was quick and easy. In between contractions she fancied she could hear the boy singing, a high clear sound that soothed her.

Settled in bed with her newborn son, she called for the boy. He came and stood by the bed. She watched him as he stroked the baby's head and was startled to see that tears had filled those great blue eyes and were spilling over on to the downy head of her son.

She said, 'I love you very much.' He nodded, smiled, reached for her hand and said clearly and calmly, 'Yes, I do know.'

54

010

THE HILL TOP

Jackie Macintosh

It was one of those crisp, blue, late- autumn mornings which never fail to lift the spirits. The sun was just peeping above distant tree tops and spotlighting the holly berries and gorse flowers. I remembered an old saying that when gorse isn't in flower then kissing isn't in fashion, and smiled.

I had walked briskly up the path through the trees on the lower side of the hill and come out into the sunshine on the heathland. I puffed determinedly to the crest of the ridge before turning to admire the view. My new home in Bere Regis, a small village in Dorset, was below me but fingers of mist snaked along the valley floor leaving only the Church tower, treetops and houses on higher ground in view.

I called my dog, Bob, and we came up between the gorse bushes onto the track running the length of Black Hill.

A large Springer spaniel came up to me, wriggling a greeting. I patted him and looked around for the owner. An elderly man with a homemade walking stick and wearing a large coat and flat cap was smiling at me. He touched the peak and said,

' 'ow do.'

We walked together for a way and I learned that his name was Charlie and he had been a "Bere man" all his life. He had worked on various farms in the district, been game keeper for the local estate and run the shoots.

As we made our way together along the path, Charlie would stop regularly and pull out a few crumbs from his pocket. He would scatter them on the path and watch quietly as a robin promptly flew down for his treat.

' 'e follows me every time, all along the ridge,' he said. 'Never misses.'

We met on several subsequent walks in the following weeks and I grew to admire this simple, contented man who seemed so at ease with the countryside. He told me how farming life had changed from "his day" and would stop to point at distant fields with his stick and tell me how many cows he had milked on this farm or that. He was a wonderful guide to my new environment and I was greedy to take advantage of his wealth of knowledge. He knew the local wild life: where the pheasants had nested this spring, in which den the fox had raised her cubs and where to see the Dartford warblers and many other observations which normally pass unnoticed.

He had worked with dogs all his life and I was anxious for his opinion on my new Collie. He was less than a year old but had come from a family which had considered him a play thing for the children. He was lacking in training and very lively but old Charlie said that I was not to worry; that I needed to be very strict and very kind and he would turn out "a good 'un". He spoke with quiet wisdom and instinctively I knew that he was giving me good advice.

We parted as usual where my track dropped back to the village and Charlie continued along the ridge. I wondered how far he walked.

The following week I looked for my new friend at the usual meeting place on the hill but found instead four men looking solemn with their heads bowed. Charlie's spaniel was beside them.
I greeted them, feeling curious and with a sense of foreboding.

'This is a pilgrimage to scatter our father's ashes,' said one of the men. 'He loved this spot. It has taken us a while to get together, he died six months ago. I don't think that Dad ever wanted to leave this place.'

'What was his name?' I asked quietly, feeling rather shaky.

'Charlie, Charlie Chalke.'

On my next walk on Black Hill the path was strangely empty. I was alone. I heard a trill from the bush beside me and there was Charlie's robin.

'Hello,' I said to him, as I reached into my pocket for some crumbs.

029

THE INTERVIEW
(With apologies to Charles Dickens)

Bob Hitching

The scene:

An austere-looking office near London Docks, with a brass plate, proclaiming the name "Scrooge & Marley".

(A quiet tap on the door)
'Enter.' A deep, stern voice reverberates from within.

A rather timid young man enters the room and approaches the imposing desk of a formidable-looking middle-to-old-aged man.

'Ah, you must be Robert Cratchit, applying for the clerical position here?'

'Yes, sir – but everyone calls me Bob.'

'Take a seat, **Cratchit.** Yes, you may address me as "sir" and refer to me as Mr Scrooge. I am Ebenezer Scrooge, but no-one calls me by my Christian name. My late partner, Jacob Marley (God rest his soul), would occasionally use it when he wanted to ask me a favour, not that it helped him at all.'

(He laughs.)

'But to the business in hand: You live in Camden Town, I see from your letter. How did you get here today?'

'I walked, sir.'

'Over a league in the rain – most commendable, but I trust you made no puddles in the entranceway. Now, let's see: you have a house in Camden Town. You rent it, I presume Cratchit?'

'Yes, sir, at four shillings and sixpence per week. It is so cheap because my dear wife has to clean our landlady's house and do her washing.'

'And how many children do you have?'

'We have three bonny young 'uns, sir, but our youngest, Tiny Tim, is rather weak and sickly.'

'Three! Too many for a man in your position, Cratchit. But I seem to be receiving all kinds of irrelevant information from you. So, back to the business in hand. I gather that you lost your last position due to the unfortunate fact that Smith & Sons went out of business, allegedly due to over-trading. However, my own sources have identified poor housekeeping and much-too-casual keeping of their books. Have you any comments on that, Cratchit?'

'I am sorry sir, but I could not possibly discuss the business of my last employer.'

'Quite understandable and commendable, my boy. By the way, your application is written on very high-quality paper?'

'Yes sir. Smith's had some redundant letterheads and I was allowed to have some. I cut the tops off...'

'They **gave** you this! And this was unnecessarily high-quality paper for a firm like Smiths! No further comment from me is necessary. However, while we are on the subject of stationery, I will tell you that my last clerk was dismissed because he purloined two packets of pins (Apparently his wife was attempting to augment her housekeeping by doing some dressmaking, but that is another story). Just pins, you may think, but from my experience this could easily be the thin end of the wedge, as they say. Pins, then paper, sixpences, crowns, sovereigns! Nip these practices in the bud, I always maintain. You understand, Cratchit?'
'Fully, sir. You may rest assured that I would give you no misgivings in that direction should I be fortunate enough to obtain this position.'

'You are aware of the salary I am offering: A full fifteen shillings a week.

But I have to warn you that from this, I will have to deduct the cost of not only losses and breakages, but also what I would consider undue avoidable wastages of paper and the like.'

'I understand and fully appreciate that, sir'

'The hours are nine o'clock until six o'clock, nine to one on Saturdays, but in the case of unavoidable calls on your work, you would be expected to work on until the job is finished. With no extra pay of course. And in the case of, I would hope, very occasional lateness, that time would be added on to the end of the working day. Also, I expect the successful applicant to come in early every Monday to clean the office.'

'I would, of course, be pleased to do that, sir.'

'And if I now tell you that you have not been successful, Cratchit?'

(Getting up to go)
'I must thank you for giving me so much of your most valuable time and giving me the chance to apply for this enviable position, sir.'

'Not so fast, young Cratchit. I like your reaction, so I am offering you the position on the terms we have discussed – starting tomorrow. Do you accept?'

'I do indeed, sir. Thank you very much.'

'One last thing: I will tell you in confidence before you actually become my employee, that Ebenezer Scrooge would like to be remembered, even after a hundred or more years, as an example of judicious husbandry, frugality and meticulous economy. There, boy, you would not expect an apparently hard and strict employer to have dreams, would you? But if you catch my coat-tails and hold on to them, the name of Robert Cratchit, too, could become synonymous with me and my ambitions.'

'I understand, sir. Thank you and good morning, if I may be so bold, Mr **Ebenezer Scrooge.'**

(Scrooge laughs)

'I admire your spirit, Mr **Bob** Cratchit. Until tomorrow – nine in the morning, sharp.'

WHISKY ANGEL

Sharon Jones

She awoke to a room full of shadows. She lay still for a minute, listening to the deep breathing of other party goers who had apparently crashed out in this room too. She could make out body shapes in the gloom; sprawled across the floor as if dropped there. Her head was pounding and her tongue felt thick and dry. How much had she had to drink? She tried to remember. She had vague memories of almost passing out in the hall and being brought in here by a younger guy. Josh? Josh with the quiff. God she hoped nothing had happened between them. This was becoming too much of a habit. It was at least three days since she'd slept in her own bed. She was starting to miss it. Were her flatmates even wondering where she was?

Suddenly she wanted more than anything to get out of there. She needed another drink. She found her shoes under the bed and carrying them in one hand she crept out of the room and gently shut the door. After a few minutes she found the lounge and picked up her jacket but her bag was nowhere to be seen.

'Fuck,' she whispered to herself. She downed an almost full leftover glass of wine and left the flat.

The stone steps leading down inside the tenement were icy cold on her feet but she didn't dare put her shoes on, not that she could have managed the stairs in her heels.

The old main door creaked loudly when she opened it; the noise scraped across her skull echoing the pain inside her. She winced, 'Not again. Not that. Not now.' She stood squinting in the afternoon daylight, letting her eyes adjust.

'Did you say something there, love?'

The voice came from a huddled figure in the next doorway. He swigged from a bottle as he watched her. She walked over; the sweet smell of whisky reaching her before she even sat down. They leaned into each other for warmth and without a word he handed her the bottle.

She answered him after a few minutes of his watching her, in silence.

'I said, "Not again".'

'Not again, what?'

'Fuck, I don't know. All of it; me, this bloody city, the daily shit. You know what I mean?'

'Yeah, I do. Try living on the streets.'

She didn't know what to say to that, but she didn't need to say anything because right then he started talking. He told her his story and as he spoke she heard her own sadness; saw her own pain reflected in the depth of his eyes. This stranger was no stranger.

In a rush to tell each other their stories they kept up a continual river of words, it meandered around them and embraced them. It sheltered them from the cold slanting rain as they walked through the streets of Edinburgh. The city was home to both of them; they walked the streets following the map of their memories, reliving and sharing. She thought how sad it was that all of their happy memories belonged to the past.

Finally, tired of their wandering they settled on North Bridge to watch the sunset over the castle. They sat side by side, both of them with their legs dangling over the side. The castle looked magnificent lit up against the violet sky. The Scott Monument stood tall, its proud silhouette standing watch over the gardens below, the birds singing their evening song. She had often sat like this. The bridge felt solid beneath her, unmoving and strong.

'This is the one place I feel safe.' She started, wanted to explain to him how the ancient castle and the history of the place held her here and made her feel secure.

'I could sit here and look at this view forever...'

'Why don't you then?'

'...Sorry?' she laughed. 'I have to go to work and besides the police would move me on. I wouldn't get peace to sit here like this through the day. People would think it was weird, they'd probably think I was gonna jump off.'

'Have you ever thought about it? Jumping, I mean?'

The air paused between them. Her whisky-addled brain tried to make sense of what he had asked.

'Yes,' she said looking him straight in the eye.

'Me, too.'

She knew he had before he even said it. She knew him, they were the same. He was ready to leave this behind. They both looked down at the street below them, and then back at each other. There doesn't have to be a tomorrow, she thought. No day at the office for me trapped in the grey corporate world. No streets and humiliation for him. We could both be free. Her heart soared with the idea. They finished the whisky and tossed the bottle behind them; then, heart hammering with excitement, she grabbed his hand and they jumped.

***

The next day, police were busy cordoning off Market Street and removing the bodies of two young people. The headline in that day's Evening News would read: "Drunks Jump to Death in Tragic Suicide Pact". If they had looked up they would have seen the outline of two figures, sitting on the bridge holding hands watching the golden shades of a new dawn warm the sky.

'Forever,' he whispered, and she smiled.

041

DATE OVERDUE?

Mike Lawrence

Samantha had worked in the library for five years. At twenty-four her colleagues constantly nagged her to have a regular relationship. Sport occupied all her spare time. It kept her looking fit and slim. Maybe today was going to be different. A young man stood at the service desk, with a mop of fair hair and light blue eyes.

He was close to Samantha who was collecting up returned books with her back to him. She jumped when he asked her for help.

'I'm, um, sorry.' He stammered, 'but I can't get this book to scan. I've tried several times, er, but I can't book it out.' His face turned bright red even under the stark fluorescent lights.

'Don't worry. I'll do it at the desk.' She took the book and his card, turned and walked across to the counter. The girls behind their desks smiled at him, and then looked at Samantha, and in unison each raised an eyebrow. She mouthed *'What?'* at them and then tugged down her black jumper over a short tartan skirt worn with navy blue thick tights. She might have been wearing a greasy overall, he wouldn't have noticed, he was concentrating on her pretty face.

'There. Sorry about that.' She smiled trying to be friendly yet professional. 'You'll have to bring it back to the desk when you return it. There are still a few rogue books about. They're probably like me, afraid of computers.'

'You idiot,' she thought, 'what an inane remark, he'll think I'm a complete dork.'

As she handed him his library card Sam noticed his name, 'Mr P Marchant'. Desperate to learn his first name, all she could do was guess; would it be Paul or Peter? She watched him leave the library with a huge smile on his face. Yes, he was her type, six foot, clean shaven, expensive jeans and a blue checked shirt she would have chosen for him.

Behind the counter Liz prodded her in the back with a pencil. 'Well?' she asked pointedly.

Samantha replied, 'Well what?'

'Oh, don't pretend you haven't got the hots for him, you go dippy every time he comes in."

'Don't be daft. Look, outside, there.' She pointed towards the window. 'He's with his wife or partner, whoever she is, and baby plus a toddler. I'm not *that* desperate.'

***

'Do you want another coffee, Sam?' In the back office Liz and Maggie were being "Mum".

They had spent their lunchtime cajoling their young protégé to date "Mr Right" or more precisely, "Mr Marchant".

'You know what, you two are like a couple of agony aunts. Shall I just blurt out, excuse me Mr M. can we go to the pub for a drink tonight, or are you busy? Busy looking after your two children; but there again I expect your wife might not approve. I understand."

'So you're quite sure he's married then?' Liz looked at Maggie who quickly turned her head away, diving behind her Hello magazine.

'Seen his family with my own eyes. How much more evidence does anyone need?'
Samantha tried to sound pragmatic but it sounded like a police statement.

'Oh, for pity's sake, Sam, look him up on the system, you know his name.'

73

'I couldn't do that. Besides isn't it a sackable offence?'

'Even if it was, who's going to tell on you? Certainly not us.'

Maggie's voice came from behind her magazine. 'The only way we want to get rid of you is to see you married. I'll be retired by then anyway.' She daren't look Samantha in the face. Not wanting to give the game away.

***

'Do you know?' said Philip, 'I have never been in this pub before, ever.'

'It's nice. I like it here. The girls at work come here sometimes after work or for somebody's birthday. They recommended it. Said the food was really good and value for money, too.'

Samantha tried to relax, as she always wittered on aimlessly when nervous. This wasn't the first time out for a meal with a man, so why on edge? Maybe it was the first time with a great looking guy and every female under seventy eyed him up as they passed. It made her feel warm inside and her tummy danced up and down.

'So, do you like being called Sam or Samantha?' He leaned forward across the table and there was that fresh, citrus deodorant again.

'Oh, my close friends call me Sam; only my mother kept to the long version. She's funny that way, insists on calling Dad, 'Michael' when the whole world knows him as Mike.'

'Wish he wouldn't look into my face like this. It makes me feel I'm falling into those lovely blue eyes.'

'Well, what do you say, Sam?'

74

'About what?'

'Would you like another drink or wait and have wine with the meal? It's up to you. I shan't have any more alcohol now. I'm saving myself for later.'

'Why? What's happening later?'

'I'm driving, of-course. Unless you want to walk home!' Laughing he topped up her glass and went to fetch a menu from the bar.
Sam sipped her white wine and thought about Liz and Maggie.

'Really, those two scheming little minxes, they ought to wear pointed hats and have warts. Didn't tell me they had looked Phil up on the computer and knew he was single. No wonder they kept on at me to make a date.'

***

Philip bent over the pushchair, stuffing shopping into the tray underneath.

'There you go, Vicky. Where to next?'

'You don't have to come. I'm only popping into the Co-op for some nappies. Aren't you meeting Sam today?'
'Later, she's working. I'm on day off so I don't mind helping. Besides young Karl needs someone to keep him under control or he'll have everything off the shelves!'

Three year-old Karl attempted an escape but Philip swept him up and held him aloft. The toddler giggled, he loved playing with his uncle.

75

DILEMMA

Bob Hitching

Bob was in a dilemma. He had never been in such a position before and was really torn as to what to do for the best.

The problem was quite simple. He had written this short story some time ago and knew it was certainly more than just good. It was, he believed, though he modestly would have hesitated to claim so in public, truly brilliant. Definitely much better than anything he had written before.

He knew exactly the market it would suit, so had sent it to the publication he had in mind more than two months ago. He was aware that this monthly in particular received dozens, if not hundreds, of submissions every week and they were notorious for sitting on both the "possibles" and the "probables" for ages.

So Bob had also recently sent the story, after a few small revisions, to a local short story competition - nothing wrong with that: It was fiction, original, his own work, had a title, and had not been published...yet!

However, and I am sure you are ahead of me and have already guessed what happened. Yes, the monthly now accepted the piece and asked Bob for a few brief details and a photo of himself so that they could print these over the story, introducing him as the author. This was on the very same day he received an invitation from the competition judges to attend the readings of the short-listed submissions. So he was obviously in with a real chance to win their prize, which was incidentally worth more than twice what he would receive for publication of his masterpiece in the monthly.

What to do? Of course Bob could have kept quiet about the acceptance of his story and it would be published in due course after the competition was closed. But he felt that would be morally wrong and could not go along with it. Even if he later claimed he did not know about it when the contest was judged. However, he _did_ know and could not live with that. So the choice: He had to withdraw his story either from the monthly or from the competition.

He asked his wife what she thought and what she would do if it were her problem. But Marie told him exactly what he would have said if the positions were reversed:

'You have got yourself into this fix and only you can decide, Bob. It wouldn't be much help or indeed fair if I told you what I would do. But I do know you, my dear husband, and I will write down how I think you will decide and seal it in an envelope for you to open when all this is over.'

Poor Bob, he wanted so much the expected kudos for his story in print and yet also would dearly love to win the competition. And that lovely prize, of course!

I suppose, in theory, he could have thrown himself on the mercy of the judges and explained the position to them, but his piece would probably then, in all fairness, have been considered "not strictly original" anyway.

So Bob did what you probably would have done - he withdrew from the local competition.

As it happened, a genuine consolation was that he would not have won, he was told in confidence later.

And they had given him his £2 entry fee back!

As for Maria's sealed envelope, 99% of ladies reading this piece will know the answer: She was absolutely right. Yet I expect only 50% of men will have guessed correctly what he did. Let alone what Marie had forecast!

Still, after all, does it matter? This is just a story...OR IS IT??

035

ES IST HEUTE EINFACH NICHT MEIN TAG
(It is just not my day today)

Charles Kirkby

I wake up in the morning as usual and I turn to my bedside table, grab my tobacco pouch, take note of the numerous warnings slapped on the side about cancer, impotence and the fact that it will be much harder for me to get pregnant. Although all of this is assumed as I buy directly off the boats (which saves me about twenty five pounds a month from the cost of duty-paid tobacco and, so I am told, makes me a terrorist), the French government could be telling me the cure for cancer for all I know.

Cigarette finished I switch on the HiFi, remembering of course the manufacturer's advice that 'turning this product's volume up to its maximum may cause 'irreversible inner ear damage', although it does get me thinking about the damage caused by straining to hear the damn thing which is now at the (hopefully) 'safe' decibel level.

After this I begin to get dressed into my work clothes, taking care not to iron, boil wash, tumble dry or burn said items I then walk to the kitchen where I am greeted by my Polish flatmate, I greet her in Polish, ask how she is in Polish then return to my native tongue to ask if she would like a coffee. I then ask whether she has any allergies to caffeine which the product may or may not contain, satisfied that no harm will come to us I add some sugar (taking note of my recommended daily allowance) and continue to the fridge only to be affronted with the dilemma of having no milk.

Breakfast is put on hold as I walk down to the local supermarket where I buy a family sized box of Crunchy Nut Cornflakes (which contain traces of gluten, wheat and nuts) and some milk (which may not be suitable for those with a lactose intolerance and may contain traces of dairy). I pay for my items and walk past the newspapers and after a sideways glance at 'The Daily Telegraph' I discover that there is a 'High threat of terrorist attack' posed by either the IRA or the Taliban, sufficiently terrorised by this apparent threat I run home wondering to myself what happened to ETA? They were all the rage when I was growing up. I then drop off my purchases, remembering to bend at the knees and not the back, and head to B&Q.

Whilst there I buy some sheets of MDF (which I soon discover could cause irritation to the lungs from prolonged sawing) and a packet of nails (which may have sharp edges) I pay for my things, receive a plastic bag (which could cause suffocation if given to a child, should always be recycled and not flushed down the toilet) to deposit my things and a free coupon for twenty five percent off my next purchase (not in conjunction with any other offer).

As I get home I begin the task of boarding up my windows, watching closely for any splinters that may become a hazard, once finished I settle down to my cereal and (now) milky coffee. I switch on the news and an informative little article about the cancerous properties of most household items resigns me to the fact that I need to throw away all of my cleaning products, rip out my television antenna and burn my sofa.

So I am sitting on the floor writing this to you with my coffee in a shatter proof beaker (noting the warning that the contents may be hot) researching the cancerous tumours that may be caused because of extensive periods on laptops.

Google is as good as ever, I have 5,586,897 hits in 0.37 seconds (and yes, Google, I did mean cancer not cacner), so I have decided that this will be my last note, that I will stop eating meat (as too much has been proven to cause pancreatic cancer) and that I will stop using all technology asap. So have made my last phone call (It was to my boss to say that I will not be coming back as it is not good for my overall chances of survival to be around that many sick and elderly people) and all that's left is for me to say is 'goodbye I'm off to read some books on philosophy', after all no harm has ever come from a Nietzsche-reading vegetarian...

Actually I might go sit in my flat mate's room; I can get a better overview of the whole flat from there.

FIVE ON A PLATE

George Chambers

Charlie straightened up, muttering 'I'm sure the bloody weeds are getting stronger every year'. Then for the nth time that day he surveyed his allotment. His best effort yet. It was mid-June. The weather had been good and he was set on winning a prize at the County Show. He and his mate Harold in the next allotment competed with each other. All he needed was a good display.

He enjoyed the disciplined nature of the presentation. A friend had showed him the trick of a good display. Have good stock but don't display everything at once. Vegetables can look dry and sad. That costs points, keep some under the table for replacement. 'Let the judges see it decorative, add a bit of parsley'. This became a standing joke between Charlie and Harold. 'Five on a plate and a bit of parsley'.

He planned showing early vegetables and prize sweet peas. He also had some carnations in his greenhouse at home but he kept those as a present for his wife on their anniversary.

The allotment was his pride and joy. He had devoted himself to it ever since they lost Julie at the age of five from meningitis. He had cried for ages but his wife hardly shed a tear. 'She's being stoical,' His mother told him. 'People come to terms with that kind of loss in different ways. Leave her be and she'll come round.' That was ten years ago. Nobody recognised depression. "Pull yourself together" did not work and Mary dealt with it herself. It took a lot of courage but she got a job as a dinner lady at the local junior school. Charlie had his job on the railway. They had their holidays and life seemed to settle down to some kind of normality.

Today Mary told him that she was going to the WI with Harold's wife for a talk on flower arranging. 'I'd like to do an arrangement with your sweet peas for the County Show. We can't always ask my sister to do it'. He said he did not mind but he would have to select and cut the blooms. He then went to the pub with Harold.

They had slightly more to drink than usual but were not drunk. They left the car in the car park and staggered home. On the way, Mary and Angie came running down the road towards them. 'Charlie. Charlie.' Mary threw herself at him. She spoke in gasps. 'We've been burgled I've called the police.' They silently hurried home.

Statements, finger prints, pictures of damage, and assessment of loss made. Charlie protested at the finger prints. 'It's for elimination purposes, sir'.

'It's a targeted job,' the police told them. 'They knew what they were after and had been quick. What we call an in and out. They were after antiques.' That set Charlie's mind racing. He was now stone-cold sober - or so he thought. He did not know any antique dealers. But did he? He said nothing.

Not a lot of damage. The front door had been forced. But the display cabinet had been left open.

'They've taken my whole Clarice Cliff tea service that was left to me by Grandpa Davis. Oh,Charlie. Look.' Mary pointed to the floor. 'They've broken Julie's doll.' This keepsake had been in the cabinet and lay broken on the floor. Charlie swore but Mary said nothing. .

Somehow or other they got through the night.

It was just after five in the morning when there was a loud banging on the door. 'Charlie. Charlie'. It was Harold.

'It's the allotment, Charlie. You've just got to see this. The police have been called on the mobile.'
 What now? Will it never end, Charlie thought.

'They ransacked the allotment,' Harold said breathlessly. 'Everything's gone! Lettuce, cabbage, broccoli, cauliflower, courgettes, carrots, parsnips beetroot had been dug up and stolen. Only the runner beans had been left standing.'

Charlie's dahlias had been trampled; marrows and pumpkins cut. The debris was all over the place. Worst of all, his sweet peas had been stripped. About a dozen other allotments had also suffered.

'Market Traders,' called Charlie. 'I'll get the bastards.' He grabbed a spade that had been dropped and fled. Realising his intent the police sped after him.

Harold slouched home. He did not know where Charlie was.

'He's at the Police Station,' Mary told them. 'They have asked me to bring some spare clothes. Will you come with me? What do they want his clothes for?'

Charlie sat in the corner of the strip cell in nothing but his underpants. He'd torn his clothes up threatening to hang people with them.

'We had to put him in there, Mrs Adams, for his own sake. He was like a wild man. We have never seen a man so consumed with rage. He may be charged with criminal damage.'

'Charlie?' Mary was kneeling beside him.

'Sorry love - I lost it,' he replied. 'I'm alright now. Let's go home.'

They never found out who stripped the allotments but Mary's elder sister and her husband were arrested for burglary. They stupidly had left the tea service in their shop. Mary did not want it back. Charlie took the broken doll away. The CPS gave Charlie a caution.

In the middle of the July, at the County Show, Charlie entered from his own garden but did not win anything.

However he did get an "Artistic Achievement" Award. He had taken five pieces of the broken doll, placed them on a plate with some parsley, their wedding photograph, and in the centre Charlie had placed an old-fashioned milk bottle filled with red carnations from his garden. He called it 'Resurrection'.

When Mary saw it she put her arms around Charlie's neck and cried and cried and cried.

GIDDY-UP, BUTTERCUP

Valerie Morris

Philippa Kendal-Smythe is a slender, elegant sounding name. Ms Philippa Kendal-Symthe was standing in front of a full-length mirror in her spacious bedroom and, as she gazed at her naked form, she was forced to admit there was one thing she was not, and that was slender.

Running her hands over her ample curves, prodding a little here and pinching a lot there, she exhaled a soft sigh. Her reflected shoulders shrugged back at her as she reasoned that you could not expect to be a wisp of femininity if you were born the daughter of a six foot five, eighteen stone rugby player and a lady who was reckoned to have the best seat in the county when she rode to hounds. Recognisable from one hundred metres they said.

Picking up her clothes from the king-sized, reinforced bed which she had recently purchased from Harrod's special orders department, she encased herself in her underwear and slipped into a loose Indian cotton dress. Then she fastened her size nine sandals onto her solid feet and left the room. She wandered into the farmhouse kitchen and set about preparing a very full English breakfast, sniffing the smells like a Bisto Kid. Long ago she had dispensed with diet books and calorie-counting and enjoyed her meals with gusto.

Taking her mug of coffee out to the yard, she felt the warmth of the morning sunshine caressing her. It was not yet hot, but promising the best of an English summer day. Her father appeared from the byre, where he had been helping sluice down after the birth of the latest addition to his internationally famous pedigree beef herd.

'Hello, Buttercup!' he exclaimed - this being the name by which he had addressed his daughter since she had been three years old, golden haired and, even then, fond of huge wedges of butter on her bread. Her hair had never darkened and along with her merry, brown eyes was one of her attractive features.

'I'll fetch you a coffee, Dad,' she offered. They stood shoulder to shoulder and sipped their drinks as they admired the view over the fields to the distant hills.

'Oh, Buttercup, I'm not sure if I told you that I'm expecting an important visitor this week - well, today actually?'

'You did say someone from one of those vast ranches they have in America, would be visiting us. Is that who you mean?'

'That's right. I received a letter, only yesterday as it happens, might have been delayed in the post. Anyway, he's arriving this afternoon. So, will you be here 'cos I have to go out until this evening and your mother is helping Janice at the stables, they're short handed.'

'That's fine Dad, I'll be here.'

Mr Kendall-Symthe heaved a sigh of relief.

'Good, good, and I can rely on you to make him very welcome, show him anything and everything he wants to see, right?'

' 'Course you can Dad.'

'Big money involved here, Buttercup, so best foot forward, heh?' He playfully slapped her rump as her returned to work.

Philippa went back upstairs to check that a room had been prepared for their visitor. Satisfied that towels were provided and everything spick and span, she decided to pick some flowers to bring the summer day indoors. Her mother phoned to say she wouldn't be home until around seven, so she made lunch for herself and her father. Afterwards, when she had cleared that away, she decided to do some baking, not being sure what time their visitor would arrive or if he might be hungry.

She had removed two trays of scones from the oven and just put in a

93

cake when the door-bell rang. Wiping her hands on her apron as she dropped it on a chair, she hurried to the front door, which she opened to reveal the visitor.

Mr Brett Harvey Nellis was a fitting representative of his home State of Texas. Philippa was well aware of this as she discovered that she needed to look up into his face. The breadth of his chest and shoulders shut out the light. He doffed his hat and smiled down at her with a perfectly managed set of American dentistry.

'Good afternoon, Marm. I'm looking for Mr Kendal-Smythe.' At the same time his blue eyes sparkled with appreciation and the realisation that he was looking at a woman whom he'd thought he'd never find. What a woman, a real armful of curves and cute dimples, even on her elbows. Brett Harvey Nellis, who was well-known to many airlines because of his need to book two seats to accommodate his person, found that he was hoping, quite fervently, that he might need to book four seats for the return journey!

'You've found the right place. I'm his daughter, Philippa.'

'Allow me to introduce myself, Brett Harvey Nellis, Marm. I believe I'm expected?'

'Yes of course. Come in Mr Nellis, I'll show you to your room.'

'Please call me Brett,' boomed Mr Nellis as he followed Philippa's rounded rear up to his room.

They spent the next hour or two viewing the house, the farm and the herd. They found themselves less and less inclined to talk business and more and more about each other. And, after a much appreciated tea of Philippa's scones and cake, Brett Harvey Nellis' admiration reached fever pitch. The warmth of their mutual affection grew by the minute until it seemed only fitting and right that they should put the Harrods bed specifications to the test in a blaze of mutual admiration!

After all, Mr Kendall-Smythe had asked his Buttercup to look after their visitor, be welcoming, and show him everything he could wish for!

023

GOODBYE, WILF

Bob Hitching

Old Wilf was on his last legs. He had been really ill and bedridden at home for some time.

'Still, I made it to the grand old age of 78.' he told his wife, Lily - as if she didn't know! The doctor, whispering, had told her that it was very unlikely he would survive the night, but Wilf had heard it from his bed - nothing wrong with his ears, even if everything else seemed to be letting him down!

He wasn't grumbling though; he had held down decent jobs most of his long working life; had enjoyed his twelve years of retirement; had a happy, if maybe a rather quiet home life, with his Lily and their two children. Then there were the four grandchildren and three great-grandchildren (so far!). Though he didn't see much of any of them nowadays as they had all moved away.

Wilf's hobby had always been consumer competitions. Way back, he had been quite successful, in a small way. He had never won the car he really, really coveted, but prize holidays in Paris and New York had more than made up for that. In those days there were mainly slogan and complete-the-sentence contests - he really enjoyed the challenge of those. But nowadays there are just prize draws, with a simple question to answer to get round the law. He was never lucky at all with these, but not through lack of trying!

He used to enjoy doing crosswords, too (especially prize ones!) but now claims, tongue-in-cheek, that the clues are printed much smaller and the cryptic answers are more difficult!

Many years ago, however, Wilf had achieved a really decent win on the football pools - enough to give them the deposit on their first house - but no large pay-out in the fifty-odd years since. Just a few minor dividends!

He still remembered when everyone used to say, 'When I come up on the pools...' Today it's always, 'When I come up on the Lottery...' Yes, he himself had said both of these many, many times.

He had won a few tenners from Camelot, but that was all. Nothing at all from his couple of hundred Premium Bonds, though.

However, he still believed that one day he would hit the jackpot from *something*. It had kept him going!

So it was with a real thrill and feeling of satisfaction to be told by Lily on this, his very last evening, that she had just received a phone call from Camelot telling them that, thanks to his bank standing order, he had won just over £2 million in last Saturday's lottery.

But when Wilf looked into her big blue eyes, he knew she was fibbing, so he told her: Good try, dear, but...If this were a fairy story, Lily, I would believe you and the news would buck me up so much that I'd recover from the illness.

'And if this were in a novel or short story, then I would have been convinced by you and died happy and contented.

'Or, if this were in a movie, good news from Camelot would actually come through tomorrow, after I have gone, whether or not I had been taken in by you, Lily.'

He thought for a moment.

'But this is real life (and death, too!). I cannot try to pretend to believe you, but your thoughtfulness and consideration is worth more than any monetary prize. A truly great gesture - thank you, dear.'

With that, Wilf closed his eyes, saying, 'It's goodbye time now. Don't bother to try and wake me, love.'

So Lily didn't and, trying to hold back her tears, she kissed him and let him be.

Therefore, this is truly...

GRAPES AT BEDTIME

Anne Petersen

Grapes hang heavy on the vines over the path, the air is sweet with their sticky juice. Wasps gorge themselves on the aromatic flesh, too full to sting, too busy to buzz me as I walk bare-headed beneath them.

My right hand reaches upwards for the jointed handle, that little point in the vine branch from which the bunch descends, hovers next to a particularly well-formed bunch, flicking it backwards to break the stem. My left hand moves into place, cupping the fruit, waiting for its surprisingly heavy weight to fall.

Saliva swims into my mouth, anticipating the dark wine flavour as I cram in three grapes at once.

Heaven. This is what I've missed, the unforgettable, indescribable taste of our own grapes – the grapes we rescued from a tangled growth of trees, bushes and weeds. This year I'd say our grapes are pretty good.

The memories crowd back – this isn't what I'm here for.

Suitcase abandoned, I run up the porch steps and open the heavy old metal door calling Rick's name. But the rooms are silent, secretive. I go through each in turn, my hot feet dampening the smooth tiled floors.

Rick should be sitting at our kitchen table, thinking, concentrating, looking up as I kiss his forehead, rumple his hair. I feel his invisible presence, smell a lingering memory of his cigarette smoke in the still air.

I move to fill the kettle with the bottled water left from last time. But it won't be fresh, it's been months – my hand freezes mid-way. Hesitantly I try the tap. Water flows.

I make tea, absent-mindedly pour a mug for Rick. I'm not sure whether this is helping, or not, but I had to come back to Bulgaria to find out, try to find out what happened, where he is.

Everywhere has memories. The whole house shouts his name. From the day we viewed Petrovo, it was his decision to buy, his ideas we worked to. Planning the bathrooms and kitchen, choosing the units, finishing off after the builders – all his.

***

I sip my tepid tea, take in the view from the back window. Our fields, our barns, the countryside beyond.

Dusk settles silently on the purple hills. In another minute blackness would swathe the landscape, at least until moonrise. I sit and watch, drink more tea, then go back out into the cool night to reclaim my suitcase from the insects. And pick some more grapes.

Bedtime. I leave the hall light on. I need its reassurance before tiredness takes away my memories.

***

Morning. I awake to the sound of cockcrows, cold air on my face, see the pale voile curtains flickering against the windows. There must be a wild east wind. I watch ripples of light playing on the walnut tree's gnarled branches and glossy leaves – no woodpecker today, only the hawk sails the skies. But the sunshine freeing itself from the clouds is warm, it'll be hot by noon, reach a peak mid-afternoon, cool down by evening.

I'm trying to think but questions crowd in. Where was Rick, why had he disappeared? Had he lost his money, his mind? Was he still alive? Unlikely, but yes, I was sure – wasn't I? So what should I do next?

The plan is to tidy up the place, and then sell it. Is that what I want? I look round the room. The bedroom windows look back at me. The frames need painting. The builder had left them and gone. I need paint.

***

The road to town is treacherous with potholes. I drive slowly out of the village and across the bridge. Sun beats on bronze bulrushes, fires yellow ochre trees, bleaches grass. Swallows scythe the stillness, test-runs for the long haul. Distant fields are patterned with rows of workers.

I make the town without incident. Parking's not a problem except on market day. Today I stop right outside the bank.

Will the card work? Can I remember the pin correctly? Rick's birthday, backwards. I can't forget that. There's someone looking over my shoulder. I hunch over the keys.

'Six, eight, one, three – backwards is three, one, eight, six, okay?'

Rick's voice, the hairs on my neck stand up. I daren't move my head.

'Punch it in.' A pause. My mouth is dry; I don't remember how to breathe. I turn round. An outline, a shadow, a pale image of Rick slips away from my eyes leaving empty space.

The machine buzzes. I press a key and out comes a mini-statement. We're still in business.

* * *

The hardware shop is busy, as usual. The owner, Boris, recognises me and smiles. I produce my list.

'Hello Boris. You have paint, brushes?' I mime and he laughs, produces several to choose from. At last I have everything.

'Rick?' He's remembered the name and smiles, pleased with himself.

I shake my head, forgetting that Bulgarians nod for no. He looks confused.

'Rick,' I start again, stop as my eyes strain to cry. But I can't. Just stand there, stupidly holding a handful of Leva. Someone turns my shoulders towards a room behind the counter. Sits me down. Gazes at me with kindly eyes. Boris's wife, I think.

I find a tissue, blow my nose and calm down. I should have expected this, prepared myself better. Rick was in and out of this shop all the time, sometimes twice a day.

Boris appears, looking anxiously at his wife and me. I can't explain, don't have the words to tell them Rick's disappeared, vanished, leaving his car and belongings on the Dunkirk/Dover ferry.

Easier to give them the official line. I put my hands together and close my eyes. According to the authorities, anyone who isn't alive and hasn't been seen for over six months could be dead. And after six years they're officially presumed dead.

GREETINGS TO EARTH

Tim Naish

We and I greet you through your radio receivers. Please do not be alarmed, we only wish to communicate and help if we can. I have studied the signals from Earth for many years and have learned your system of communication.

We are a swarm mind in a particle cloud eleven light years from you and your world. We exist in the outer fringes of a peaceful solar system where no other minds exist.

For millions of years I have studied the Universe, observing the interplay of matter and energy, seeking patterns and meaning.

'Why have you spent so much time and effort searching for meaning?' You may well ask.

All I can say is that, when you exist in a particle cloud in a stable system where little happens, there is not much else to do. So we would say 'Why not?'

When first I perceived your radio transmissions we thought they were another expression of the random events of the universe, an interaction of the magnetic flux around a gas giant with an orbiting iron meteor, for instance. We have monitored such data before and, while the patterns convey information about the processes that make the universe work, when all is said and done, it's all just more Physics. Interesting as data but nothing really new.

The first signals from Earth were very weak and hard for us to detect, but they contained a pattern that I had not encountered before, so we set a system in place to analyse the pattern. Over the course of time the signals grew stronger but increased in complexity as well, so that more processing was needed to decode them.

Through this decoding system it became evident that multiple patterns were being broadcast from sources all over the planet. We became interested beyond our normal curiosity. I considered that a being like Ourself might be trying to make contact, but we could not understand how life could exist under such intolerable conditions, in a toxic oxygen atmosphere and crushed by gravity. Perhaps the signal came from elsewhere in your Solar System and only seemed to come from the blue dot. Naturally, we looked in the cool calm outer edges far away from the harsh radiation of the star. I found nothing beyond normal background activity.

By setting more of my minds to the task, it became possible to pick out different strands in the stream of information and to concentrate only on the dominant themes. We could then start to analyse the coding contained within the transmissions. The radio waves seemed to represent a type of communication that we had not previously encountered in many aeons of existence. We thought that a being like me was attempting to make contact but we could not understand why the signal was so complex.

Perhaps the being on the planet had only recently reached a stage of development where its mind integrated enough to reach out from its environment and attempt contact.

We could not understand why, in that case, the signals were so difficult to decode. It would make more sense for an initial message to be a simple greeting or a form of basic pulses, rather than the layers of entwined transmissions that I was receiving.

We set aside a part of me to work on the philosophical implications that this issue raised but I and we do not expect any coherent answers soon.

We also set apart another part of the swarm to work on separating the various strands of the message and a further set of functions to study the physical properties of the planet itself. In order to understand the data that arrived from that area of the swarm, it became necessary to construct physical models and perform experiments using rocks and gas from some of the bodies within the system.

In studying and decoding the various frequencies used we found that different sets of coding were being used on different transmissions. Also, the different sets of coding seemed to depend on time and on the position of the planet. A report back from the section of our mind given the task of studying the physical properties of the planet gave us the answer. Different regions of the planet's surface were emitting signals in different codes.

We did not understand this until I and we began to reintegrate a few of the minor sub-minds and found that they had developed some new communication tools and terms of their own for specialised purposes. It was much more difficult to bring these lesser minds back into phase with Ourself, almost as if they had developed into separate entities and were resisting reintegration. We realised that given sufficient time and a certain amount of carelessness, communication between different parts of the swarm could become more difficult, perhaps even impossible. This could eventually lead to a complete mental breakdown.

Has this happened on Earth? Distressing as it may be, the evidence seems to point to it. The personality of the planet had broken down through some misadventure, so that by the time we received your first weak message there may have been as many as 100 individual minds on the planet all with a different personality.

The strengthening signal and increasing complexity are all symptoms of the same thing; a mind turned against itself screaming out for help as it literally falls apart.

Even now the number of minds on Earth may have reached the thousands, each of them isolated from all the others, all of them wanting help. I and we cannot tell which of you can understand us or wishes to communicate, so We must address you all.

If there is anything I and we can do to help you, please let us know. The distance between Us and You is too great for any physical contact but sometimes it helps to talk.

For now We only have one piece of advice.

Earth, if you are listening, pull yourself together.

HEARTS AND POPPIES

Kathy Sharp

The Reverend Pontius always fancied himself as a detective. He had, or so he thought, just the right turn of mind for this sort of thing. Incisive. Penetrating. And a terrier-like grip on the problem in hand. Not that he would have said so aloud, of course. Goodness, no. Heaven forefend. But in his idle moments it was good to have something to work on, something to occupy his mind. Use it or lose it, thought the Reverend.

There had been a surprising number of mysteries on the island lately, particularly since he had been visiting Mother Culver, the Keeper of Stories. The stories were all fine and dandy, of course, island histories — but it was the collection of prophecies that interested the Reverend Pontius always fancied himself as a detective. He had, or so he thought, Reverend. Mother Culver's archive of stories and prophecies, all mixed up and disorganised, were encased in her head. And it was the Reverend's unwavering intention to prise them all out again, sort them into order and write them down for the benefit of all. At least, that's what he told himself.

Mother Culver, on the other hand, prized her wonderful, and alarmingly accurate, prophecies very highly, and was reluctant to part with them. She tended to let them out on a slow drip feed. Very slow, sometimes. Indeed, she had recently kept one of them to herself until after the event it foretold had actually taken place. But she had her own very good reasons for that. In his darker moments, the Reverend suspected her of witchcraft. But then, she was an islander, and he was an off-comer, and they were never going to properly understand each other. But he had, he simply *had* to know more of the Archive.

And so it was that the Reverend Pontius trudged across to Mother Culver's hovel one keen spring morning. The wind, thinking it was still winter, tried to make off with his hat and made his ears burn red with the cold, so he was thoroughly cross by the time he approached the old woman's hovel. There would be no warmth or comfort there, he knew, and he longed for his cosy room under the bell-tower. As a matter of fact, he preferred to sit outdoors when he visited Mother Culver. The thought of being enclosed within four walls with her made him profoundly uneasy, and he hoped she would come outside to speak to him.

'Here comes that nosey parson again,' said Mother Culver softly to herself.

'Come to steal my Archive, he is. Thinks I don't know it. But I have his measure, never fear.'

She had known he was on his way long before he appeared at the end of the path. Useful information of that kind just popped into her head from time to time. He wouldn't come indoors. She knew that, too. So she went outside.

'Good morning to you, Mother,' said Pontius, his numb fingers feeling in his top pocket for the little brandy flask he had brought for her. He liked to think of it as a gift, but it was actually a bribe. Payment in kind for a verse or two of the Archive. She snatched it out of his hand before he could offer it, and secreted it in some hidey-hole inside her shawl.

The old baggage had no manners at all, thought Pontius. She was insufferable. Irritating. But she did have the prophecies, and they had all come true, so far. So he said nothing.

'You'll be wanting a History, Reverend,' said Mother Culver, knowing perfectly well this wasn't the case. She just enjoyed baiting him.

'I'll be wanting a useful prophecy, Mother. Something that hasn't already happened, this time, if you please,' said Pontius, firmly. He wasn't going to be messed about by this old crone.

She didn't reply, but went straight into the trance-like state that she seemed able to call up at will. Pontius waited, poised to memorise whatever she sang. He was getting quite good at it these days:

> *Come the strangers, seekers of the key,*
> *Every ship and heart they mean to break;*
> *Beware the hornèd poppy of the sea,*
> *The freedom of the island is at stake.*

Mother Culver stopped. Was that it, then, wondered Pontius? The exchange rate of one verse of prophecy to one flask of brandy these days was pretty steep, he thought. Still, there was plenty to think about here. The old woman waited, daring him to demand more, but the Reverend was already on the case.

Now this key, thought Pontius, fancying himself as an interpretative expert on the Archive, is it a real object, or merely a symbol of understanding? Mother Culver watched him beadily as the thought ran across his face. He tended to wonder if she was reading his mind, but in point of fact his expression was always completely transparent.

'It's a real key, Reverend,' she said at last. 'Golden. Long lost.'

I really wish she wouldn't do that, Pontius thought. They're so damned deep, these Islanders. There's no working out what goes on in their heads. But he didn't think it for very long. His attention was deep in the scrap of prophecy. The part about ships and hearts was clear enough, wasn't it, if a bit disturbing. But what was all this nonsense about hornèd poppies? How could a flower threaten the freedom of the island? He turned and walked away without a word, engrossed in these juicy new mysteries.

'How rude,' muttered Mother Culver to herself. 'No manners at all, even for a parson. And, as usual, he has stamped off without waiting to hear the rest of it.'

But the Reverend Pontius was gone, both in person and in attention. 'I shall solve this conundrum for the sake of the island!' he said, gallantly. But deep down in an unacknowledged, shadowy corner of his soul, he knew that he just enjoyed playing the detective. And off he went, happy, with his head full of hornèd poppies and broken hearts.

HIT THE ROAD, JACK

S. J. Scally

Jack Jones turned the car off the country lane and drove carefully through the gate which hung precariously on one hinge. Tutting at the sight, he parked up and turned off the engine.

'We'd better leave the car here and get our wellies on. Don't want to get her muddy.' Jess hopped out excitedly and threw open the boot of their pristine car.

'I can't wait to see how it's looking, can you?' She leant in and tugged out their boots and jackets. 'There might even be some walls.' Neither of them had been to the site of their new house for a fortnight but they had been reassured by Pete, the site manager, that everything was right on track. The completion was expected in two months and Jack couldn't quite believe it.

They slipped and skidded their way up the muddy track and as they crested the hill they both gasped and stopped.

'I know what you're thinking.' A voice to their right made them jump. 'I've been waiting for you to turn up so I could explain."

'But...'Jack's mouth moved, but nothing else came out. He gawped at Pete, incredulous.

'You...' Jess seemed to have caught his affliction.

'I know, I know.' Pete raised his hands in a gesture of surrender. 'You must remember it always looks worse at this stage of the build.' He spoke very quickly, so that they couldn't interrupt. 'It might look like nothing's happened since you were last here...'

'Well, what has?' Jess screeched, rounding on him.

'What has what?'

'Well, what has happened?' Her voice had become high-pitched and she took a step towards Pete. Sensing danger, he took a step back.

'Um,' Pete cleared his throat, stalling for time. 'Well, let me see. I've organised the cement for the foundations. That's due this week. I've recruited Archym and Kasmir to help. That's them there. They're working on the trenches.' He pointed over to where two pale, middle aged men sat in camping chairs, smoking and drinking tea.

'Hey,' he shouted and waved at them. 'They're just having a break, you know. It's tiring work.' Jess sniggered then glared at him.

'Now, now, Mrs Jones. They've been working like real troopers they have,' he looked offended and she thought she saw his three chins starting to wobble.

'We were lucky to get them.'

'So, back to the schedule,' Jack tried to appear conciliatory. It would do no good to have the two of them at war with each other. 'Foundations? This week?'

'Yeah, then we'll start the building next. Say, a couple of weeks for the walls, three at most. The roof, one week. Make it watertight, always helps, dunnit?' Pete laughed, but was met by two pairs of eyes staring, un-amused, back at him. 'Um, yeah, so then we start inside.'

'And that's all still achievable in two months?' Jack watched as Pete shifted from foot to foot then stroked his chins, deep in thought.

'Two months?'

'That's what the schedule says.'

'Does it really?' Pete whistled through his teeth. 'Phew, we were being hopeful weren't we?' His chuckling was stopped abruptly when he saw Jess's thunderous face.

'Well, obviously we'll try our hardest.' He smiled at her then turned on the charm. 'I don't want to be here any longer than necessary, believe me, Mrs. Jones. But, if I'm honest I'd say two and a half, maybe three months. I'll know more next week once the foundations are done.'

He folded his arms and stood with them resting on his beer belly and not for the first time Jess wondered whether it would make her feel any better if she just throttled him now.

'So, we're talking about the end of August for us to move in?" Jack spoke to break the tension.

'August?' Pete counted on his podgy fingers. 'June, July...yes, suppose you're right, August. That doesn't sound that far away, does it?' He glanced at Jess, trying to keep his voice upbeat and positive, but she wasn't fooled. She'd seen fear in his eyes and it filled her with doom.

'It sounds extremely far away to me,' she replied, her voice low. 'I want to be in my own home.'

Pete spotted an opportunity to change the subject and took it quickly.

'Oh? Mrs Hubble not looking after you properly?'

Jack's eyes flicked a warning to his wife and he laughed nervously.

'Oh your sister is lovely,' he stuttered. 'It's all fine. We just miss...' He wanted to say: "We miss food that doesn't resemble cardboard," or "We miss bedding that doesn't make your hair stand up with static," but being English and therefore not at all assertive he simply replied, 'We just miss having our own place.'

Pete just nodded in sympathy.

'I agree. There's no place like it,' he said, slapping Jack a tad too hard on his back. 'You'll be in yours, here, September at the latest. How's that sound?'

037

LADY IN THE RED ANORAK

Mike Lawrence

Katherine pushed open the door to her local library. She would choose one book today as she hated lots of books lying around her little flat. Something romantic perhaps, she mused; turning left and then straight down to the Fiction shelves. Katherine could find her way around in the dark if need be. An avid reader and one of their best customers.

Booking out *The One You Love* by Samantha Gresham, she crossed the road outside and walked down towards the Country Park. There she would sit at the back of the park's café, enjoying a pot of tea and reading her book. There were others in the café, but it was nice to do a bit of people-watching at the same time.

There was an art gallery displaying local artists' work so there was always plenty to occupy a couple of hours until lunch time. After that she would walk around the park and feed the ducks.

'What a sad life I lead,' she thought. She had been on her own since Mother had died twelve years ago. Still in her mid-fifties it would be great to have some male company sometimes.

She drained the last of the tea, closed the novel and left the café to wander down the grassy slope to the House. In a sheltered spot in front of the Georgian façade Katherine sat down on a bench seat. This was where she had first met Donald, a lovely man about her own age, struggling along with his dog, Sandy. That poor, old dog, its back legs stiff from arthritis and weak from old age. It looked as if its owner had to tow him along.

At this first meeting, Katherine had joked, 'He could do with a skate board; that would be easier.' They both laughed. That was it, she didn't realise it straight away, but that was the moment cupid had pinged his arrow.

After that, they frequently met at the park and sometimes in the library. He also was a keen reader but preferred books on English naval history and real sailing adventures. Having been in the Merchant Navy he had a natural interest in anything nautical. She loved his conversation about his trips and visits to many countries around the globe. But all this was soon to end.

Katherine continued to visit the park and its café but 'one man and his dog' as she called them were nowhere to be seen. She tried the same time, same day and even hung about in the library. The assistants asked if she needed any help. They thought it strange because usually the "friendly lady in the red anorak" quickly chose one novel and left.

The weather during January forced her to sit inside the café drinking tea or coffee. To prolong the visit she often stayed for lunch, but still no sign of Donald and Sandy. Katherine had mental images of Donald standing in the vet's with a limp canine friend draped across his arms; their very last visit. It would be a blessing to put the dog out of pain. Actually, that was exactly what had happened.

She continued her walk through the park looking at every man on his own with or without a dog. Worst of all she didn't even know his surname or where he lived; no mobile or home phone number. Nothing.

***

A week later Katherine was back in the library. What will it be today? A novel, perhaps, or something historical for a change. What series did Donald love? Alexander Kent was the author and he told her they were fiction but based on true life aboard seventeenth century square riggers and the exploits of the British navy.

Knowing her way about the shelves made finding Kent's series of adventures on the high seas easy but the top shelf presented a challenge to a woman of five foot one. Luckily she was able to grab the only book left by this author with her finger nails.
On her way out she received a strange look from the librarian

wondering if the "little lady in the red anorak" was losing it. Why had she gone off romantic novels?

The short stroll down the main road seemed longer than usual. When she reached the gates there was a fleeting moment when she thought, 'I don't think I'll go in today.' Same old paths, same café, and probably same old people.

'Oh, well I've nothing else on, might just as well,' she thought, perking up as she remembered the different book in her bag. Somehow reading a subject that Donald knew and liked would bring her some comfort.

'A pot of tea and a slice of Dorset apple cake, please.' she asked the young girl serving at the café. 'Yes, for one, thank you.'

That last reply hurt a bit. Sitting at the back, as far away from the door as possible, she turned the book over and read the synopsis on the cover; definitely not her scene. A story about a young Captain involved in the American War of Independence. It might be great once you've got passed the first chapter or two.

She concentrated on the apple cake and poured another cup. 'I'll start reading it tonight in bed.' Looking out of the window across the wall garden and to the lake beyond, she knew she would never see Donald again. A tear slipped down her cheek.

Standing up she stuffed the book into her bag. It was then that a small white card fluttered to the floor, falling like a sycamore wing, rotating and slowly drifting downwards. At first Katherine imagined it had come off the table. She bent down and picked up what was obviously a business card. It had come from inside the book; used as a bookmark by the previous borrower, it could only belong to one person.

Donald Whittaker, Upton Court, Blandford Road, telephone number 07970 207688.

MESSING ABOUT ON THE RIVER

Janette Nourse

In silent flight the owl turned for home as the first rays of morning pierced the sky, slicing down through a thick covering of morning mist which edged the grey estuary water. The death-cry of his last prey alerted the chicks nesting in the nearby barn that breakfast was coming. The water's edge awoke with each shimmer of morning light as it caressed the covering blanket of mist; a lone vole scurried, weaving in and out of the long grass adjoining the reed bed.

Safe in his vantage point, the fugitive, alerted by the brightening morning, stretched first one leg, then the other easing them into a more comfortable position. The bustle of the river was building, each bird trying to gain its allotted space along with so many others. Wagtails, distinctive black and white feathers standing out against the pale morning, were pecking and bobbing for any choice morsel along the bank. With equally inky black plumage, Moorhens broke the cool river water, ripples of their wake slithering across the surface to mark their progress.

Concealed, the fugitive felt safe in the knowledge he would not be detected. A stupid mistake had led him to this spot in God knows where; he was angered by his own foolhardiness. He had become tired and exhausted by the persistence of his pursuers. Each time he thought he was safe they were on to him, and he had to move on again until he was unsure of which way to turn. He could not stay in this safe haven much longer as he needed to find something to eat and gain strength to escape far away from here.

On a sandbank, further out in the estuary, two herons were fishing, their impossibly spindly legs somehow enabling them to balance as their gimlet eyes searched for signs of breakfast. Soon several hapless fish had been dispatched down the herons' elegant throats, their beaks pointing skywards. Their hunger temporarily sated they simultaneously took flight to search for richer pickings a little way inland. The nearby houses overlooking the estuary had many ponds filled with fat fish irresistible to the two canny anglers. They made the fugitive remember his own hunger; he would have to chance being seen and break his cover.

The sun rose in the sky, its warmth burning off the veil of mist still suspended above the shimmering waters. The temperature brought out myriads of insects, clouds of them replacing the mist above the water's surface, their numbers so dense in places they formed a fine gauze layer. The sun's rays silvered the ripples of the water beneath and caught the metallic wings of dozens of dragonflies; each one frantically flapping through their day in the sun before eventide marked their early demise.

Dozens of squawking gulls above drew the fugitive's eye skyward as they ventured inland after juicy insects. Swirling and spiralling, each bird appeared to be on a collision course but at the last minute arced up in a totally different direction making an elegant loop. Golden fingers of sunlight kissed the gulls wing tips as they performed their aerial ballet, their precision and flair, choreographed by nature. How he envied them their bravado and freedom, the sky was theirs, they were not bound to the earth but free spirits to come and go as they pleased. Far from his home and companions he was hunted and afraid of discovery.

A small boat butted up the shallow waters of the estuary loaded with visitors toasted by the sun's rays to a lobster pink. Each one had powerful binoculars and expensive photography equipment, long lenses at the ready to capture the moment.

Voices drifted on the warm breeze, 'Herons, British Grey Thrush, and a rare North African Blue Starling.' Each name was punctuated by dozens of camera shutters clicking in unison.

He gazed at the boat full of "birders" smugly ticking off each sighting they had earmarked on their must-see lists. The chugging of the boat and the fragmented commentary drifted off along the estuary. All was peaceful, even the noisy gulls had departed. The fugitive realised all the birds had fled as, like a rapier, a hunting bird flashed across the horizon on the lookout for his next prey. The falcon's movements were precise, coldly calculated and controlled. His economy of movement preserved his stamina for a speedy kill when required and it would be a lucky bird indeed that could out-fly him once he had them in his sights. A naive young gull, unaware of the danger he was in straggled after the retreating body of his flock and soon paid the penalty for dalliance.

The falcon disappeared as quickly as he had arrived, his mission accomplished. Gradually the birds returned to the estuary and the happy bustle of messing about on the river recommenced. All above was a whirl of feathers and flight, the sun warming ruffled feathers and giving them a polished sheen against the bluest of skies. Infected by the carnival atmosphere the fugitive ventured from his hiding place, stretching his legs, hesitantly flexing his shoulders, stiff from inactivity. Then he too was soaring, the sun bringing out the burnished blue of his feathers. He swooped low over the estuary as the chug-chug of the boat's engine heralded its return.

A dozen shutters clicked simultaneously, binoculars at the ready, eyes, straining to glimpse the "Rare North African Blue Starling". He gave one last victory fly-by to please the crowd and then headed towards the setting sun. Perhaps he would find his flock and once more become one of the crowd; he'd had enough of the limelight. Far to the south his group of North African Blue Starlings attracted little attention as they found roosting space amongst others of their kind, hundreds strong.

MIRRORS

Diana Holman

Pausing momentarily on her journey up Market Street, Pam glanced into the windows of Debenhams. Drawn by the colourful display of Spring fashions that had just replaced the January sales, she stepped into the doorway to look more closely.

As she studied the elegantly clothed figures, her attention was caught by the reflection in the glass of a dark blue Mondeo making its way up Market Street and drawing to a halt on the double yellow lines further up the street. The driver stepped out, and after a searching glance up and down the length of the street, he sprinted across the road and disappeared into Clinton Cards.

Pam would have known that man anywhere, even though it must be thirty years since she saw him last. The dark hair was peppered with grey now, the waistline had got thicker but it was unmistakeably Barry Stevens. The Mondeo carried no "Barry's Better Driving" boards, so he must have retired now, Pam thought.

She smiled to herself. It was ironic she should catch sight of him in a reflection, when his fixation had always been with mirrors.

'Use your mirrors,' he would bark at Pam.

'Women don't know anything about mirrors except for this,' he would add disparagingly, miming passing a comb through the dark oiled hair, and running an imaginary lipstick over his fat lips.

He wouldn't get away with it these days, Pam thought to herself. Women know how to stand up for themselves now. He might not have got way with it so easily then if she had not been only seventeen. The driving lessons had been a birthday present from mum and dad. They had chosen Barry's Better Driving because it was a small local firm, more personal, mum thought, and half the price of British School of Motoring.

On her fourth lesson, she had come out of a T junction a bit tight and had scraped a car parked on the kerb. Barry had rung her father from a call box and told him he had better come down quickly as his daughter had been involved in an accident.

Poor dad had run all the way, with dreadful visions of mangled wreckage and blue flashing lights, so it was almost a relief to find it was only the door trim on a Ford Anglia that had been ripped off. Fortunately it happened outside Dorothy's house. Dorothy had been in the community play with Pam the year before, so she made them all a cup of tea and said that it was the sort of thing that could have happened to anyone, and that the car had been parked far too near the junction.

It was nearly always reversing that caused the problems. After one of Barry's explosive tirades about using her mirrors, poor Pam would get in such a panic she couldn't even drive forwards, leave alone backwards, and the car would bounce along as if it had a kangaroo in the tank instead of the Esso tiger.

In the end, even Mum and Dad had had to acknowledge defeat and ring up Mrs Withers at the Flying Colours School of Motoring. Mrs Withers just laughed and carolled,

'Never mind – no damage done!' as in panic on her first lesson, Pam sailed out in front of a large lorry, missing it by a whisker amid great screeching of brakes and swearing from its driver. Mrs Withers just gave him a cheeky wave out of the window. Once Pam and Mrs Withers got laughing together, Pam soon forgot her nerves and passed her test. I bet Barry's forgotten to buy his wife a Valentine's card, and he's having to rush in and get one at the last minute, Pam thought with a grin.

Slipping out from the doorway of Debenhams, she marched purposefully up the street. There are times when your job gives you real satisfaction, she reflected, adjusting her hat with its chequered brim. Stepping firmly round to the front of the Mondeo, Pam took a couple of brisk shots of its number plate with her digital camera before starting to write the Fixed Penalty Ticket.

MOVING ON

Jenny Grant

Jane stood in the kitchen enjoying her first coffee of the day. She looked out of the window at what promised to be a beautiful day. Jane could take no pleasure from it. She sighed deeply. The truth was her daughter, Kim, and she were not getting on – and it hurt.

'Oh, don't go on, Mum.' was all she seemed to hear. She felt herself nagging her daughter not to make a mess, not to make so much noise coming in late.

'I don't mean to go on, Kim, but I think you could be a bit more considerate.'

It was her house after all! Kim earned good money; she could afford to get a flat of her own, but Jane didn't dare suggest it. She loved her daughter living with her, perhaps she could have coped with this better - but for the letter she had received yesterday. The results were in. She had to see her consultant. She hadn't told Kim of the worry she was having - time for that when she had to.

That night she opened her heart to Bill. He was a kind man. They had met a few weeks ago at their art evening class and it was now a habit to go for a drink afterwards.

'She needs a place of her own, Jane, she is too comfy at home, can't you drop a hint?'

'It is her home, I would never turn her out.' Jane was looking so upset that Bill changed the subject.

'How about we have a day out on Sunday? Drive to the country, have some lunch.'

'Oh, Bill, that would be lovely.'

'I won't be home tomorrow, Kim, get yourself some lunch.'

'Oh, Mum, I had asked Ann for Sunday roast, she'll be upset, especially as she is on her own now.'

Jane liked Ann. She felt that she was a good influence on Kim. Perhaps she wouldn't go after all.

That evening Bill phoned. 'All ready for tomorrow?'

'No, Bill, I'm sorry, I'm not feeling too well. I think we'll have to make it another time.' She couldn't tell him the real reason.

'Let's leave it until tomorrow. I'll ring you in the morning.' He sounded disappointed.

'I'm off, Mum, won't be late, I'll tell Ann it's okay for tomorrow.' The door slammed, Jane sat staring at it.

'No "Thank you, Mum"' she muttered, it was all taken for granted – so she would be spending another Sunday in the kitchen.

She heard Kim come home later. Heard her music go on. She had Ann with her, they were making coffee. She heard Ann say:

'Turn the music down, we'll wake your Mum.'

'Oh, Mum sleeps through anything,' laughed Kim.

In the morning Bill phoned. 'How are you feeling?'

'Much better, are you still on for today?'

'You bet.' She heard the pleasure in his voice. 'What time shall I pick you up?'

'Give me an hour.' That would give her time.

Going into Kim's room she gave her a prod. She was under her duvet, lost in a deep sleep. She woke with a start:

'Oh, Mum, what on earth are you doing? It's Sunday, what do you want?'

'Just to tell you that I'm going out after all, the food is in the fridge.' She would never forget the look on Kim's face; she was completely speechless; something that rarely happened. She went out and shut the door.

She had a lovely day with Bill. He was so happy to be with her. She felt comfortable and would like to see more of him. As he dropped her at her gate he brought up the subject of Kim.

'How are things with your girl? It can't be easy.'

'I would love you to come in for a coffee but I don't know what the atmosphere will be like.'

'Leave it, Jane, but I do think you must sort things out. It's your home after all.'

 He was right.

'Bill, will you come for dinner tomorrow?'

'Will it be alright?'

'Oh yes, it certainly will be fine, and thank you for a lovely day.'

He put his hand on her arm, his eyes were soft.

'Let's hope it is one of many.' Jane had made up her mind. She didn't know what was in store for her. She was determined to make the most of every moment.

Kim was watching TV when she walked in. She didn't bother to look up. She said nothing. Jane went upstairs, had a long hot bath. Going into the kitchen she called back:

'Do you want a sandwich, Kim?' There was a grunt which she took for a "yes."
She made them one each and handed Kim a plate.

'I'm having a friend for dinner tomorrow, someone I would like you to meet.'

'Well, I won't be here,' snapped Kim. 'I have other plans, I know when I'm not wanted.' With that she flounced out of the room and slammed the door.

Jane felt her eyes filling. Her lovely daughter who had brought such joy from the day she was born. Now they were hardly on speaking terms. She often wondered what would happen if she met someone. It was six years since Dan died. She knew that she was ready for someone in her life, but how would Kim react? She wanted to welcome Bill into her home, but it had all been spoilt.

Jane woke early and heard Kim leave. She had hoped she would look in to see her. She loved to hear her usual: 'Bye, Mum, see you later, have a good day' - but that hadn't happened for some days now.

Jane kept herself busy preparing the meal. She tried not to think about her visit to hospital the next day. Just keep strong and look forward to seeing Bill this evening.

The doorbell rang on the dot of seven.

'Hope I'm not too early,' he smiled, handing her a beautiful bunch of flowers and a bottle of wine. She, too, had made an effort; candles lit, a real fire and lovely smells coming from the kitchen.

'This looks wonderful, Jane,' he said, making himself comfortable by the fire. They made easy conversation, laughing and feeling relaxed in each other's company.

The meal was a success. They were sipping their wine when Jane heard the front door close. She jumped up.

'Excuse me Bill, I need to talk to Kim, I didn't think she was coming home until later.' Bill looked uncomfortable. He hoped he didn't make things difficult for Jane by being here.

'Hello, Kim, I didn't think you were coming in till later.'

'Why, Mum? Isn't it convenient? I do live here. Anyway I have something to tell you, but I will keep it until you are not too busy.' She glared at Jane. 'I'm going to my room.'

'Oh, please come and meet Bill, he will think it so rude, he is looking forward to meeting you.'

'Well, I don't want to meet him, but - two minutes - and then I'm off.' She flung open the door and stood in front of Bill. Suddenly her face lit up.

'Mr. James, what are you doing here?' she smiled.

'Well, we meet again, Miss Fox.' Jane was speechless. She looked from one to the other. She had so been dreading this moment.

'I met Mr. James in his office this afternoon and he was so helpful.'

Jane stared at Bill.

'What office?'

'My old place of work. I help out there when they need me.'

Jane sat quickly down. Her legs suddenly seemed weak.

'What's going on, Kim?'

'I will leave you both to talk. Jane, it has been a lovely evening, I will see you at class tomorrow.' He laughed. 'Don't look so worried, everything will be fine.'

'Kim, you know Bill?' Jane's face looked mildly accusing.'

'No, Mum, Ann and I have decided that we're going to share a flat. We went to the nearest estate agent in our lunch hour. He was so helpful, in fact I found him very easy to talk to. I think the time is right, Mum, don't you?' She came over to Jane, put her arms around her.

'You and Bill will be our first dinner guests.'

'Kim, I have something to tell you.'

'What is it, Mum? Just tell me.'

'I have to go to hospital in the morning. I have had tests, I have to get the results.'

'Oh, Mum.' She was crying now. 'You never said a word. What has happened to us?'

She took her mother in her arms. 'I'm coming with you.'

'You don't have to, Kim.'

'Oh yes I do. At least I can try to make it up to you. I have been so selfish. If there is anything wrong with you I'll never forgive myself.'

The next morning they went to the hospital and both drew comfort from being together.

'Well, Mrs. Fox, I'm pleased to say that your scans were clear. We will keep a check on you, but I hope I won't see you again.' The man, in whom she had such faith, was smiling.

'Thank you so much.' She shook his hand. The relief was so great that she could hardly breathe.

'Now, Mum, I've got a surprise for you. I'm taking you to see our new home. Bill has arranged it. I think he will make a lovely stepdad, by the way.' They both laughed heartily, arms around each other. Jane felt so happy. It was wonderful to have Kim back to her old self. A friend as well as a daughter.

MOVING ON

Janice Kirkby-Brown

Sarah sat listlessly at the kitchen table. This had been the biggest mistake of her life. She smiled at herself. She was going to say "So far", but having already achieved her biblical three score years and ten Sarah couldn't imagine the rest of her life affording her that much opportunity to make many bigger mistakes! Why had she allowed herself to be persuaded into moving here?

It had been such a wrench leaving the old Town House that had been her home since the day she married 50 years before. What would Frank think? Or his family? The house had been his family home, the home he was born in, that his family had lived in for generations.

The family's first house had been a humble affair in the early 1800s, a basic two-up, two-down in a small terrace of similar properties. As the family, and their fortunes, expanded it had been built up, extended, neighbouring properties bought up and the whole thing remodelled. She and Frank had traced it back over five generations, the planning applications, architect's drawings, electoral roles, photos, parish records and where available the Census returns. "Reverse-architecturing", they'd called it - tracing back the impact each generation had had on the building until they could see what the original must have been like.

Later they'd gone on to trace his family tree, all the way back to the time of Queen Elizabeth. The First Queen Elizabeth. Ironic that the beginning of her reign marked the end of their quest. Even if Frank hadn't got the big 'C' and left her alone, they could find no earlier family records. And now with Queen Elizabeth the Second his family name would end. Another irony – just as they gave up any hope of having children, Jeannie had come along. Trouble with daughters is they move away to marry into their husbands' family, just as she had all those years ago.

Yes, and then just because you're getting older and struggling a bit with the stairs they talk you into selling up and moving into the garden basement flat of their husband's country pile. You end up miles from anywhere: no-one to talk to, nothing to do and totally dependent on lifts to get back to any real semblance of civilisation. What's the use of a bus pass if there's only one bus a day either way?

Sarah looked at the potatoes Jeannie had given her yesterday. They were in a thick, dirty, brown paper bag.

'Dig yourself a patch.' Jeannie had told Sarah. 'Anywhere in the garden will be fine. Plant yourself some veg. I thought maybe you could start with these.'

Sighing, she grabbed the bag and the gardening trug – another present from Jeannie containing gloves, kneeler and trowel all in matching 'garden green' with an equally green radio sporting a daisy aerial. Leaving the radio behind, Sarah went out into the garden and wandered aimlessly down the full length of it and halfway back before settling on one, random spot just to the side of the lawn.

Throwing down the kneeler she sat on the ground and started digging as best she could. As she dug Sarah shook her head but she couldn't help smiling. Did Jeannie really think you could dig a whole vegetable patch with just a hand trowel? She must look like some elderly archaeologist scraping the soil away in tiny clumps to search for artefacts, not a serious gardener trying to plant potatoes!

Even as the thought formed in her head, her trowel unearthed the edge of something lying in the ground. Carefully she moved away the soil like she'd seen them do on TV, then used the tip of her trowel to ease it out and into her hand. A little wooden doll, with a one broken leg. Definitely not something belonging to her grandson. Actually it looked too old to belong to her daughter even.

The doll was roughly shaped and pinned together, the kind of doll she remembered seeing when she was a child. It was in a bad way, and had obviously been in the ground a long time. Sarah took it into the house and cleaned it up as best she could. With the dirt gone you could just make out the crooked smile somebody had given the doll, maybe when it was first made or later, when its original face had worn away.

Sitting at the kitchen table her initial elation over finding the doll began to wane. Her first thought had been to wonder who had owned the doll, but here in this house she had no idea. Jeannie's husband was also an only child, so there were no immediate candidates. If she were in her own home, in town, Sarah knew exactly what she would be doing right now - heading to the Record Office, checking the Census and Parish Records to find out who had lived in this house in the past, and whether they had children. She would be looking for a little girl who had lost her doll.

She picked the doll up again and in the act of doing so another thought struck Sarah. Over the years of researching Frank's family home she had come to know the staff at the Record Office so well they'd taught her to use the computers. Surprisingly Sarah had enjoyed the new technology and volunteered to help transfer records onto the system so they could be accessed on the Internet. Her friends often joked that she was more Granny Geek than Silver Surfer, but she'd never had a computer of her own. Maybe if Jeannie really wanted to buy her a present, she'd ask her for a laptop, with wireless broadband and webcam so she could do some research – and maybe Skype her friends while she was at it.

MR MEAN

Bob Hitching

Bob had never been a likeable sort of person. For one thing, he had always been so terribly mean with money, and had often proved himself to be a nasty deceitful piece of work in both business and in personal matters.

You just could never completely trust him. And he had got, if possible, much worse as he got older. Everyone wondered how his poor wife, Gill, had put up with it for so long, especially on the pitiful allowance he grudgingly gave her. Privately, with her parents, she called him Mr Mean, because he was *really* mean in more ways than one. And it had always been even more so, when it came to her. Originally, before they were married, her father had been taken in by the confidence of this young man, who did not throw his money about, like most of Gill's fellow-students. Her mother had reservations from the outset (female intuition?), but he could be <u>so</u> charming in those days.

Again, Bob was so set in his ideas and could brook no argument. People had always called him - behind his back of course - for he displayed a vicious temper; A Mr Know-it-all or these days, Mr Google, for he knew everything - or rather, thought he did.

No matter the subject - Corporal Punishment ('The cane didn't do me any harm.'); Politics ('If I had the opportunity to run the country...'); The Economy ('Of course, they have got their priorities completely wrong.'); Crime ('We are too soft by half.'); The Immigration Policy ('Or lack of it!'), etcetera, etcetera, etcetera...He always had the answer.

Even on occasion when he was proved to be indisputably wrong (or not completely right, at least), then this was obviously a case

150

of the exception proving the rule, according to Bob.

No subject, however trivial, was safe from his obstinate opinions: For instance, he had always maintained that all prize draws and the like were dishonest.

Only friends or relatives of the promoter every saw any worthwhile prize.

Gill had almost given up arguing and dissenting with him, but occasionally she dared to query his unsubstantiated opinions. For example, she had today asked him why he was so sure about the prize draws - he obviously had no proof at all to back up his categorical statement. But Bob would not even listen: 'All fiddles, Woman, they are all fiddles.

So "Woman" dropped the subject. It would never be brought up by her again. And she refrained (and had great pleasure in doing so!) from telling Mr Mean that she had this morning received £25,000 from Reader's Digest from their latest draw.

And she *never would* tell Bob of her good fortune. After all, why should she, as she later asked her father (who is, incidentally, the Managing Editor of The Reader's Digest Association, Inc)?

NOUGHTS and CROSSES By Malorie Blackman

A Book Review
Licia Hitching

5 stars

Noughts and Crosses is a romantic story about two young people from different worlds who fall in love with each other, but their family disapproves of their liaison and tries to stop it. Will the young couple listen? No! They started as friends - very close friends., but their love for each other could not be ignored.

The young couple are complete opposites as the boy, Callum, is white (a nought) and the girl, Sephy, is black (a cross). Callum is poor and has just got into a regular school, whereas Sephy, whose family is rich, had always gone to a good school. They both hated what was going on and wished for peace until they became older and gradually grew apart. But...was their love for each other destroyed?

The story takes you on an exciting rollercoaster, questioning your pre-conceptions and pulling on all the emotional strings. It will make you re-think how judgemental people can be and the prejudice people face on a day to day basis. The book will bring a tear to your eye! *Noughts and Crosses* makes you realise how strong love can be and Malorie Blackman demonstrates her literary skills in her beautifully written descriptive passages, not fearing to use strong language where appropriate.

Noughts and Crosses is one of the most enjoyable books I have ever read and I guarantee it will make you see things from a different angle. So gripping is the narrative I couldn't put the book down. It will make you regret it ever ends!

OUR DAILY BREAD

Janette Perkins

Mrs Lewis had ten children. The three older boys worked down the mines, the youngest was eight years old. Food and feeding was the focal point of Mrs Lewis' day. From dawn till dusk she toiled in the kitchen. Indeed things were so hectic sometimes that she was not even baking her own bread.

There was no need anyway as there was a baker in the village. He was a hard working Italian called Mr Obortelli. He had emigrated to the valleys of south Wales in the 1920s and had established what was by now a thriving business. While he baked, his rotund cherry-cheeked wife worked in the shop. His two sons, Luigi and Stefano, before school, delivered bread on their rickety framed black bicycles. The brothers worked harder than most children back then, not only were they the delivery boys, but they became out of necessity, linguists. Most of the villagers spoke only Welsh then; English was understood, but Italian was indeed a foreign language. The boys communicated through hand gestures and head nodding. Bread and baking boomed.

As there was an absence of a Mr Lewis, and many mouths to feed, the baking of bread was substituted for the taking in of washing. This paid well, and was far more effortless than kneading. A copper full of washing required minimum amount of attention - a bit of stirring now and again perhaps. Granted, it did not smell as wholesome as newly baked bread, but freed up time.

It all began when bread was being delivered next door to Mrs Lewis. She asked Luigi if she too could order bread on a daily basis. So her name was written carefully in the blue book which he kept in his frayed top pocket of his too small jacket. LEWIS was not difficult to spell, not like that of ABERNETHIE two doors up. Luigi, took the stubby pencil out of his pocket, and licked its tip. There was a permanent blue stain on the end of his tongue. He painstakingly wrote her order on the dog eared page. 'I collect the money every Friday' he said.

As there was no delivery van, the boys went backwards and forwards to the bakery like bees bringing back nectar to the hive. The villagers could have gone to the bakery themselves, but as it stood at the other end of Ystalyfera, it was just a walk too far, besides there was free delivery.

Mrs Lewis bought the largest loaves available. She really needed extra gigantic miners' appetite-sized loaves. There was never enough bread to fill those snap tins as well as feeding those hungry ones at home. She asked Stefano one day if he would ask his father if he could make even bigger loaves. The good lady indicated the length of loaf that she required while Stefano looked on in amazement. These would be the biggest loaves **ever**!

The baker's boy duly delivered the missive. The message and request were repeated to check details and to ensure nothing had been lost in translation. At first father threw his arms up, then shrugged his shoulders then uttered sounds that probably meant - it was impossible! After a bit of thought Mr Obortelli had an idea. He would have some bigger bespoke baking tins made.

After school the following day, the benevolent baker accompanied by his two sons, visited the local foundry to see if it would be possible to manufacture these wonder tins. Yes - a few days were needed to order materials and make them according to specifications. A price was agreed — boys in translation mode — and twenty large tins were ordered.

The metallic monsters arrived -shiny and almost as big as babies' bathtubs. The baker started on his new venture with gusto. He baked one loaf and sent it round to Mrs Lewis via Luigi for approval. She came to the door wiping her hands on her apron. When she saw the prototype, she beamed, and said she would have five loaves daily. The boy rattled home on his black wheeled heap, father was delighted.

And so began several years of production. Word had spread regarding the size of Mrs Lewis' long loaves. Others wanted them too. They were easier to cut with little wastage, perfect! Mr Obortelli could hardly keep up the demand. Business was never better. Bread and jam eaten in the village had never tasted so fine.

Mrs Obortelli took the boys to Italy during the school holidays. The shop closed for two weeks. The benevolent baker still delivered each morning as he did not want to let his customers down. He made many journeys backwards and forwards to the bakery on that first day. Many paid him compliments. He did not really understand what they were saying to him, but nodded back and smiled out of politeness.

Mr Obortelli, puffing and panting and sleeves rolled up arrived at Mrs Lewis' perfectly polished door step that day. He knocked on the door and she opened it. He beamed with pride as he held out his bread basket but Mrs Lewis took a step back. There was a frozen silence. She had never in her whole life seen such hairy arms on a man. The thick brown hair spread from knuckle to elbow and was the colour and texture of a coconut. How many years had they eaten bread kneaded and pummelled by this hairy man? She had only ever seen him from a distance with shirtsleeves down. How much human hair had the Lewis Family consumed over the years? It was her duty to protect her family from this hair attack. Quick thinking was needed. She grabbed the bread, and informed the bewildered baker - in broken English - that the family were moving to the North and that no more bread was to be delivered. He smiled and nodded in affirmation. She closed the door.

008

PRETTY FLAMINGO

T Maley

A small wind blew through the leafless hedges that lined the cinder track connecting the steelworks with the expanding suburb of Warrenby on the northern fringe of Redcar. Through the dusk a group of building contractors headed for the alehouse after working on a new low-rise tower bock – all the rage in '75.

In the snug bar of the Ship Inn, huddled round two small tables next to the open fire; the lads were focused on their dominoes more intensely than usual. They were playing for the privilege of choosing a time slot for "bird watching" whilst visiting their on-site toilet.

The flats they were building overlooked a "Lunar landscape"; an open expanse of steaming ponds where the waste slag and dross from the furnaces were dumped. By some quirk of nature a Rose Flamingo had strayed in and taken up residence. How such an exotic bird got there was a mystery - perhaps it escaped from Flamingoland on t'other side of the Yorkshire Moors.

One of the labourers, Neville, loved to watch the flamingo's every movement. Old man Coulton the developer, who it turned out was a bit of a "twitcher" too, had agreed to Nev's using the loo as a bird-hide and even allowed him to use his binoculars. Earlier that morning Eric, the charge-hand, had gone in search of Nev, his "Labrador" hod-carrier. Three lifts up on the scaffold exposed to an icy sea-fret, the brickies had to keep working to stay warm and to do this they needed a constant supply of bricks and mortar and Neville was late back from break. On approaching the loo-come-bird-hide, Eric noticed Nev's binoculars, though sticking out of the top window were not trained on the flamingo pond below but upon the neighbouring flats.

'What the hell are you doing man, we're all freezing our nuts off waiting on muck, get a move on will you?' demanded Eric, hammering on the door.
Neville emerged sheepishly, and before Eric had a chance to quiz him, scurried down the ladder to fetch the "muck" quicker than a scolded

160

cat.

Curiosity got the better of Eric, and taking the giant binoculars he glassed the neighbouring flats.

'Oh my God,' he said under his breath, barely able to believe his eyes. What prompted this uncharacteristic declaration of spirituality wasn't a "blinding light", but rather a fleeting glimpse of a young woman. Although he could only see her head and upper body due to his relatively low angle of view, she was naked as far as he could tell. Frustratingly, she was facing away, towards a dressing mirror. Breathless, he watched her slip a blouse over her black bra before disappearing from view. Re-appearing, she wriggled into a woollen sweater before going for good.

'The sneaky little...' he muttered, making his way back to the top.

"Some flamingo, eh?" Eric teased Neville in the Ship that night. 'More like Sophia Loren with that yard of nut-brown hair swishing about her bare shoulders."

As Eric waxed lyrical over this newfound beauty, excitement spiralled to fever pitch. Having pumped Nev for the history of "sightings" the gang calculated the optimum viewing time was just before eleven. They agreed to restrict this "prime watch" to one man per day so as not to arouse suspicion.

As the days passed and their walls grew taller, so their angle of view improved and so too the reports on "Sophia" became more tantalizing. By Thursday Jack the "mixer-man" returned visibly shaken, his boyhood stammer having returned.

'She f...f...flung the curtains b...b...back with n...n...nothing on but a purple b...b... bra and a beautiful happy face!'

161

'You mean you saw the lot?' enquired Eric.

'Ner...ner not quite, but by tomorrow, there wur...wur...won't be much left to the im...im...im...'magination.'

'And guess who's *Friday's Child?*' Big Mick tuned in, rubbing his shovel-like hands.

Jimmy, having already had his "watch", pointed out they were progressing the job far too quickly.

'Coulton is hardly going to offer the usual Christmas bonus for an early finish if he doesn't have to.'

They all knew Jimmy was right of course, but decided they couldn't risk spoiling the chances of those yet to have a turn. Besides, Neville had promised to smuggle in his twitcher's telescope – complete with a camera attachment!

Friday morning could hardly have been a bigger disappointment. Mick returned from his watch furious.

'Just as the curtains came across that pimply plasterer Oxley started shouting and waving. She couldn't miss him and it was "game over" before it began!'

'That's the end of that then,' Eric concluded. 'Lets see if we can finish to top plate before lunch to get a "job and knock"*.

So the gang found themselves in the Ship early that Friday and it didn't come as a surprise when, to their collective approval, Big Mick landed a punch on Oxley just as he came through the door. They cheered up further when Old Fred Coulton turned up with their wages – cash-in-hand as ever. Addressing the gang, Fred's his pay-day homily took them by surprise:

162

'Just when I had you lot down as skiving loafers, you manage to finish in record time. Now don't go blowing it all at the Top Deck ** tonight boys, but I have stuck a little Christmas bonus in for you.'

As they ripped into their pay packets, Coulton strolled over to the jukebox.

'Oh no, not Dana again Fred; we can only take so much you know.' said Eric.

Fred's selection however threw them off guard. To their utter astonishment, for as strains of Manfred Man's "Pretty Flamingo" floated around the snug, who should walk in but "Sophia". They sat in stunned silence, their eyes tracking her every movement, as she headed straight over and landed a kiss on old Coulton, whereupon Fred turned to the gang, a sagacious smile slowly spreading across his weathered face:

'Now then lads, I don't believe you've met my Monica… <u>properly.</u>'

Notes
    * "job and knock" is common parlance amongst northern contractors for finishing early – e.g. especially on a Friday lunchtime.
    ** The "Top Deck" was (and is) a rather tacky night club on Redcar's sea front.

This story is fictional. However a flamingo really did "take up residence" in the slag ponds by Redcar's steel works and caused quite a stir among the twitching fraternity for some time!

22

REMEMBER ME

Olive Eastwood

She viewed her garden as she washed up; trying to remember names of bushes and flowers. How she missed her husband's loving care for it throughout the year.

But then in the past how she chided and nagged him to get on with things.

'Don't forget the wheelie bin. Hurry up or I'll be late for school. Remember you have to drop Mary off today.'

She tearfully remembered how he would sometimes say, 'Just look at those starlings in the bird bath, almost human the way they squabble'. Or he would say, 'The roses are going to be lovely this year after all that pruning.'

She dried her hands and sighed, knowing that she had set herself the task of clearing out his wardrobe and drawers.

She didn't agree with her daughter Mary, to give herself some more time before she started on it. It has got to be done sooner or later, and she hated procrastination.

She opened the wardrobe drawers and started pulling out the neatly stacked piles of underwear and packed them into the cardboard boxes that she had assigned for the task. She wondered what Oxfam did with it all?

She began with his socks and flamboyant ties, many of which she thought were ghastly. He had said once, when he thanked her for a birthday present that she had impeccable taste, though it was most conventional in reality.

At last she started on his pullovers and suits. She held up a woollen pullover ready to be folded. She never liked it really, too many smudgy looking patches in the design. Reminded him of

166

impressionist painters he used to say. She didn't think the colours worked well in wool.

Ah, now this one I gave him, he did like its heavy cable stitch. The blue matched his honest eyes, so honest he couldn't deny flirting with Phillipa at our friends BBQ when he finally took it off and gave it to her as it had turned cold. *That* one definitely has to go.

Martha blinked back the tears that were beginning to well up. No, she would not give in. She would finish the job. Six months is long enough she thought.

The suits were quite easy to deal with she told herself, as she went through the pockets. He was prone to leaving things in them. She had once found a ten pound note, but he told her he had deliberately done it.

She began folding a steel grey suit. How smart he had looked as he stood by his beloved rose bushes. They were going out to dinner. She remembered when she had picked one and given it to him, a special one the colour of a well-polished old-fashioned copper kettle. 'That's to remind you John, that I love you.' Now what was it called? She never could remember names of flowers.

She broke down and sobbed. Dabbing her eyes, she continued feeling in pockets when she did feel something. She looked down and there in her hand was a crumpled ten pound note and a dead copper-coloured rose. She tried hard to recall that moment and the name of the rose. Ah, yes, she thought, feeling suddenly very happy, as the desiccated petals floated to the ground. Wasn't it called *Remember me*?

ROMA THERAPY

Mike Lawrence

©MWL02/12

In her office near Oxford Street a young woman answered the heavy, black telephone.

'Hello, Personnel, Miss Dawn Greenwood speaking.' At the same time she was checking her blonde hair and lipstick in the small mirror on the desk. *'Why do I always do that? They can't see me.'* It was her old school friend, Isabelle.

'Oh, Issy, darling, how are you?' She used her official telephone voice. Izzy wanted to meet for lunch and have a chat. It sounded ominous. In 1958 mobiles were only seen in the fantasy Eagle comic so the two rarely spoke on the phone. Mostly because they were too busy after work being chased by young men who wore cravats and checked jackets. Both girls were rather pretty and had a line of suitors waiting to take them to parties. There were many fast rides in the country in long red MG sports cars. Their social calendars were full.

'Oh, dear,' thought Dawn, *'I hope she hasn't been careless.'*

'I'm not up the duff, if that's what you think!' Isabelle retorted indignantly. They sat at a small table in Lyons Corner House by Marble Arch nibbling sandwiches. 'You'd be the last person I'd tell anyway.' She pronounced "last" to rhyme with "lass"; being a true "lass" from Yorkshire she had a strong accent and never lost it...She slurped her tea noisily, much to Dawn's disgust, and complained about the prices.

'What is it then? Spill the beans.' Dawn was dying to know.

'I'm off to Italy. Rome actually. Next week.'

'Oh, darling, how delightful. Have you a lovely job there?'

'No, I'm just sick of London. It's dirty, the weather's awful. Look at the smog today.' She jerked a thumb towards the plate glass window. You could barely see the double-decker buses grinding past slower than the

170

huddled pedestrians.

'I thought Rome would be nicer and it's somewhere I've never been to.' She was about to swap fog for heavy rain in spring and oven hot temperatures in summer. 'Where will you stay, have you fixed anything up yet? What about a job? You're completely off your rocker!'

'Oh, Dawn, don't have a fit. You're beginning to sound like my Mum. I'll stay in a women's hostel until I land a job and then find a flat or something. The change of scenery will be good for me.'

'You don't even speak any Italian, do you? I think you are completely mad.'

Well, mad or not, Isabelle, the Yorkshire lass went to Rome, somehow got a job, found a bedsit and a boyfriend, Antonio.

Boys in those days paraded in the avenue next to St. Peter's Square. They chatted up girls over miniscule cups of black coffee, sporting James Dean greasy hairstyles and bottoms you could crack an egg on.

To start with Dawn received the odd postcard but she never expected to see her again. Fate had decreed that Isabelle would meet and fall in love with a beautiful looking Roman. He wasn't just an Italian, he was a Roman. There is a difference she was told. He was fair haired and had bright blue eyes. Not your typical Latin type, but very Romanesque apparently. To be a real Roman you had to be born and bred in the City with Roman parents.

He belonged to a respected Roman Catholic family with a business supplying the Vatican with garments and regalia. They had been doing this for decades. You didn't get better connected than that. Unfortunately, Antonio's Mama was totally against this match. 'Theez Ingleesh gal, she no speeek Italiano, she no a Catholeek, whata familia she come from? She 'as a funny accent too. No, no, no, Antonio, no marry 'er.'

Her son, part afraid of his mother and part fearful she would have a seizure, assured everyone he would "no marry 'er." He could feel his heart breaking.

Now for those who believe in Cupid, this is when he needed to fire a few extra arrows. Love-struck Antonio having explained to his English lover that marriage simply was not on the cards, heard nothing from her for several days. Unable to stand it any longer he went round to her apartment block and bumped into her leaving. She was off to pick up her ticket for a sea passage to Australia.

'You haven't ever mentioned Australia before. What's this all about?'

'Antonio, listen, there's nothing here for me. You say we can never marry. So I'm off to Perth.' She stormed off to the travel agents. When she got back he was sat on the steps blocking the front door.

'What will it take to keep you here?'

'You would have to marry me.'

A few months later Dawn received a letter from her friend. It read

> Dear Dawn, we are marrying next month. I'd love you to come over for the wedding. Wait until you see my dress! I know you would have refused anyway, so don't worry; I'm not having any bridesmaids. We get six Best Men, all lovely looking Italians. Yes I did mean six! Better bring your chastity belt. All my love for now, Isabelle. XXX"

Dawn bought the most expensive outfit she could afford from Bond Street. Isabelle's parents didn't attend the wedding, unable to find enough money to pay for the flight.

Fifty years later Isabelle stills lives in Rome. Sadly without her husband who died at an early age. Their son runs the ecclesiastical supply shop near the Vatican.

Dawn, lives in happy retirement in Dorset, sometimes flying to see her life-long friend with her luggage stuffed with real Yorkshire tea that you can't buy anywhere in Rome.

At home she gets an international call every now and then.

'Hello. Oh, Issy, darling, how are you?'

SECOND CHANCE

Jenny Grant

Fiona was late. She pushed upon the restaurant door, managing to trip over her feet. Shouldn't have worn my new Jimmy Choos, she thought. She didn't really want to be there. Later, she was going to meet Tom to talk about the wedding plans, so would have to make an early exit.

'Fiona, glad you could make it.' Tony, head of department came up. She received a quick kiss. He was fond of these out-of-hours get-togethers. Tonight though, Fiona was not in the mood for a bonding session. She made her way to the table and was pleased to find she was sitting next to Jane, whom she liked.

'A few new faces here tonight, up from other branches, I think,' said Jane, looking around the room.

As Fiona took a sip of her drink her gaze fell upon a tall, dark and familiar figure sitting at the other end of the table. It just couldn't be Dave; her heart seemed to stop. She could hardly breathe. He swung round as if he felt her eyes burning into him, then he was by her side.

'Fiona, what a lovely surprise, I wondered if you still worked here.'

'Hello, Dave. I thought you had gone abroad.'

'I did for a time, but had a good offer on the south coast, so I came back.'

Fiona's head was swimming. She had loved him so much, he hadn't changed. Eyes that never left he face, his black hair still falling over them, the way he threw his head back when he laughed.

'Take your seats everyone, let's make a start.' Tony was rushing around, waving his hands at the empty seats.

176

'We must meet up for a drink, Fiona. Chat over old times, how about tomorrow after work?'

Fiona just nodded, incapable of speech. He had been the love of her life. He had asked her to marry him, but she was afraid then of such a commitment, and asked her for time. He was hurt, and angry, and accepted a job in the South. At the time Fiona had felt he hadn't considered her feelings, only his own. But she did regret her decision, she missed him so much and now she knew she felt no different. Yet she was planning to marry another man.

She took in nothing that was being said and slipped away before the meeting had finished.

Tom was waiting for her.

'Fiona, darling, I've been longing to see you. I have good news. The vendors have accepted our offer. We can go ahead with the house,' he blurted out, excitedly. 'We can go and see it again tomorrow,'

'Oh, that's great,' she managed to say. 'But I've got to work late tomorrow; we'll have to make it another time.'

She was ashamed she couldn't look Tom in the eye. She wished she were somewhere else. She knew he was upset. I can't go through with this, she thought. I'll have to tell him. He is a good man and would give her a secure, happy life. My loving someone else would hurt him intensely.

'Tom, I have to go. Sorry, I'm very tired, ring me tomorrow.'

As she him left him, standing watching her go, she thought how tired he looked. He appeared to have lost his usual happy, easy-going enthusiasm. She knew that he knew something had happened to her, but he could only wait.

She didn't know how she got through the next day. She was first to arrive at the tiny bistro they had loved before, she was longing to see Dave again. The door opened, he was there.

'Fiona, I've been so looking forward to seeing you again, I hoped you hadn't changed your mind.'

He took her hand in his. She felt shivers go through her whole being.

'Oh, Dave, this has been a lovely surprise, I can't believe we're here together, but I must tell you something. I'm engaged to be married.'

'Yes, I had heard, but perhaps when you here my news it might change things. I'm coming back, I accepted the job today. We had so much going for us, we can't throw it away.'

Fiona could not believe what she was hearing. This was exactly what she had been dreaming about all day. But she could not understand her feeling of anti-climax.

'Dave, that's wonderful news,' she replied.

'Let's celebrate,' Dave said, jumping to his feet, pulling Fiona up from her seat.

Something made her pause and she heard herself saying 'Let's make it tomorrow, Dave. I've promised a friend a longstanding arrangement that I would see her later.'

It was a half-truth. Fiona had spoken to Tom that day and arranged she would see him after work, if she wasn't too late.

'Well, I suppose I'll have to wait. I'll see you tomorrow, and we can make plans.'

She let herself into Tom's flat, made a coffee and waited. She was surprised he wasn't at home. The flat had an empty, sad feel. She knew he had a meeting later in the day, but she would have thought he would be home by now.

She waited until eleven o'clock, becoming increasingly worried and feeling something was amiss. She was tired as well, and decided to go home. Her little cat would be starving.

At home she made herself a little supper, and she and the cat beside her curled upon the settee. But she could not eat, Tom had never let her down, nor let her worry. Something was very wrong.

She dozed off for a few minutes and was woken by the incongruously happy melody that was her mobile's ringtone. Half asleep, she grabbed at it and fumbled it on.

'Hello, is that Fiona Middleton?' said an unfamiliar voice.

'This is the A & E department at Barsetshire General.'

Now fully awake, Fiona jumped to her feet.

'Tom!' she yelled. 'What's happened to him?'

'Mr Wilson has been in an accident and is unconscious at the moment. We found your number on his mobile.'
'I'm on my way. Thank you for letting me know.'

Fiona arrived at the hospital unaware of how she actually got there. Eventually she found him in a small ward. There were six beds, but he was alone. She gazed at his dear face and realised he did not know she was there. Tears welled up and everything else that had happened over the past two days was forgotten.

She could do nothing whilst he was unconscious and was urged by the sympathetic ward Sister to go home and rest.

After a sleepless night of intense worry, she was back at the hospital just after nine o'clock. As she strode along the never-ending corridors she pleaded silently for Tom to be awake. Her joy was overwhelming when she saw him smiling as she opened the door into the little ward.

'I'm sorry, darling, to have given you such a shock. Can't really remember what happened.'

'Don't even think about it. You are alive and that's all that matters.'

Though he showed signs of being extremely week, he wanted to speak.

'You were not happy the other night neither of us was at our best. I have a problem. In fact I think that's why I lost control of the car. I have been asked to take over another position in France – I refused, of course. How could I expect you to up and leave your friends and family. You are too precious to me for you to be made unhappy.'

Fiona stared at him. Even now he was thinking only of her. How that contrasted with Dave who had expected her to welcome him back and not give any thought to her feelings and the life she had made for herself.

Tom, I would go to the ends of the Earth for you,' she laughed. 'I thought I had lost you, and yes, you will accept the job in France, if that's what you really want. How exciting, and I will be right by your side.'

Painfully, he opened his arms, and enfolded her with his love.
024

SEVEN DAYS

Clive Saunders

The seven days met four or five times a month. They'd discuss upcoming events and try to work which of them would be first and last that month.

Monday would always be first to arrive. It wasn't liked as much as the others, though it didn't know why, and rarely did mornings if it could help it.

Tuesday was a little better adjusted. It didn't crave the coffee that Monday demanded, but like the others, if not more than, it always looked forward to when Friday appeared.

Wednesday was as ever stuck in the middle. Especially when Tuesday and Thursday weren't speaking. Which was usually the case.

Thursday liked to be more aloof than the others. Never really knowing what to do with itself, or when to do it.

And of course, Friday...It often came and went with a flourish, seeming much shorter than the others, but always well received.

This only left the lazy days, Saturday and Sunday. They would always be late-rising. Though Saturday would be more frantic once it was up and about.

Birthdays and Anniversaries were discussed. Appointments made, and cancelled. The days worked well together.

Occasionally, one would take the place of one of the others. This always led to confusion, and the feeling that a day had been lost or the week seemingly to drag on.

But after the days had been together for so long, there came the nights.

They were almost always early; with the exception of Friday and Saturday who without exception were undeniably late.

The one thing they all looked forward to though, without exception, was a long holiday.

039

SHOPPING NIGHTMARE

Mike Lawrence

'What am I going to get my girlfriend for 'er birthday? Well I might find something in 'ere,' he thought as he brought his white Porsche to rest in front of Harrods.

Callum spied several girls on the pavement, they smiled in his direction and two attempted a photo of him on their mobiles. He was used to this, often being mistaken for Peter Andre, so he just waved.

'Hi, Fella, take care of 'er. Cheers, mate!' He threw the key card across and bunged George, the top-hatted doorman, the usual twenty. For that the man turned a blind eye to parking restrictions and kept the other one on anyone coming too close to the recently polished paintwork. Pocketing the note quicker than any magician, he muttered. 'Big salted so and so, thinks he owns the place.'

Normally, Callum didn't like parking any of his "pride and joys" in the street. They had all been jealously scratched so many times; the twenty pound tips were meant to keep some of the insurance claims at bay.

Once inside the store he strode quickly over thick carpet directly to the watch department. Staff smiled and nodded politely from behind their fixtures as he swept passed. They thought themselves lucky to get a grunt out of him.

Coming to a halt at the counter, Callum's eyes scanned the illuminated cabinets. Expensive? Yes, you could always tell. A large, oblong, glass tank you could float a shark in, contained just one watch delicately balanced on a clear plastic stand, lit by at least ten halogen spotlights. No price tag, of course.

''Ow 'bout that watch there?' he said pointing to the diamond encrusted timepiece.

The assistant sighed and putting down her nail file suggested it might be 'out of your league. Maybe you won't want to cough up quite so much,' she very professionally observed.

'Do me a favour, luv, this isn't even going to be my Babe's main present.' He placed both hands on the counter showing off fake tan, his fifty pound manicure and Lorex gold wristwatch which had set him back a mere sixteen hundred pounds.

At this she raised one finely plucked and painted eyebrow. Heavy false eyelashes quivered as her blue eyes scanned his stocky figure, absorbing data; the white open neck Kevin Decline shirt, Armani jeans, and Oakleaf sunglasses perched up on his close cropped black hair.

Through flame red lipstick she asked, 'Has she got this season's fragrance by David Bigham?' She was obviously reading from the poster at the side of a display.

'What's it called?' he snapped back, irritated at being manipulated by a sales assistant, especially one who looked like Lady Ga Ga in her Saturday job.

'Love in a Mist.'

She reached across for a sample bottle and tipped a minute droplet onto a paper strip.

'Would sir like a whiff of this?"

'Phew! You sure this ain't gone off?'

Sales assistant of the year shrugged.

'Hang on a mo'.' He reached inside his Diesel top and fumbled for one of his i-phones. Soon he was in communication.

'Hiyah, how's you? Great, man. Hey, David, what's the name of your

new female smelly? Oh, right, *"Snog in a Fog"*. So anything else is old stock, eh? I see, no bovver. See you at the next party, bye mate.'
He glared at Lady Ga Ga. 'I'll take the watch.'

He thrust a bundle of notes across the counter. Midnight blue and glitter fingernails enclosed the cash like a JCB grab. Then clicking away on six inch heels she headed for the gift wrap department and never returned.

Callum looked at the time and groaned. It was time to wake up. In bed he realised that today was Sharron's birthday and he hadn't bought her anything. Throwing back the tatty sleeping bag, in place of a duvet, spraying even more white stuffing on the floor, he rolled out of his pit. He stepped in a plate of last night's curry and his head started to pound.

'Oh gawd! That cheap lager in the The Cricketers dun 'arf give ya an 'ead!'

Hopping on one leg he struggled into his old pair of jeans.

'Nearly worn out, these. I'll have to get down the market for a new pair.'

He scratched around the filthy bedsit raiding jackets and pulling out overcrowded drawers trying to cobble together a few pounds. Enough, he hoped, to buy Sharron a card and a small bar of chocolate.

That's all he could afford until next Friday's dole money.

SUNSHINE AFTER THE RAIN

Moira Hawey

Oranges, that's what it is! How can anyone smell of oranges? Mark stormed out of the office. He had almost told her where to stuff the job! No wonder she was still a Miss – Miss Bloody Orange he thought. God he needed a drink!

He was angry because he knew the argument with his new boss could have been avoided if he had been more on the ball.

Consumed with anger he marched out of the building along the path towards the car park. His feet made loud crunching sounds on the gravel.

He seemed to get angry so easily these days. Why, oh why did his beloved Penny have to die so suddenly, would he ever get over the loss?

It was getting dark and the rain did nothing to improve his mood, the drive home seeming endless. All he could think about was the bottle of whisky that he would soon be opening and that would ease the pain – well, at least until the morning. Sliding a CD into the player he hoped the music would take his mind off things.

He was a tall man in good shape for his 50's, with dark hair and eyes. He hung up his damp coat, his keys clattered as he threw them on to the nearby table ready to settle down for the evening - just him, his whisky and cigarettes just the way he liked it these days. No sooner had he sat down on his old, comfy sofa when he heard a tap at the door. Penny had been his world and now that she was not here he just wanted to shut out the world and tonight was no exception.

Tap! Tap! There it was again!

Despite himself he sighed, and walked wearily towards the door annoyed at being disturbed. A small girl, with straight straggly hair and thin dress soaked through stood in front of him. She had a frightened look on her pale face as she said, 'Please mister, can you help me?'

'Do I know you, where have you come from? Please, you must go home, I can't help you, he said gruffly. He moved to close the door wanting to shut out the rain.

'It's my rabbit; I think he is in your garden.'

Mark sighed heavily. 'Where do you live?'

'Over there in the cottages,' she said shakily, pointing to the nearby houses.

He and Penny had planned to have a family. Penny had always said her first baby would be a girl and she had described exactly what she would look like. Baby blue eyes, blonde hair, just like a fairy Princess – oh! And they were going to call her Poppy. And here she was – standing in front of him now! Of course, it was not their child as Penny died before this could become a reality.

'Come in,' he relented. 'You will catch your death if you stand there much longer.' She was shivering now. He ushered her inside and pulled the throw from the old sofa and wrapped it around her shoulders.

'Does your mother know where you are?'

'Don't know,' she shrugged. 'I just went out to feed my rabbit and she was gone so I started to look for her.'

'Well, she could be anywhere now, and it is too dark and wet to go looking tonight, and not only that your mother will be worried,' Mark reasoned.

The girl started to cry.

'Look,' Mark said in a rather softer voice, crouching down to her level. 'I will search for her in the morning, first thing, I promise. She has probably found a nice barn to sleep in for the night'.

Mark grabbed his still damp coat. 'Come on, I'll take you home'.

The rain had eased as they squelched their way across the soggy grass to the old cottage.

'Do you promise to look for my rabbit?'

'Of course,' he said impatiently, eager to get back to his whisky.

With that she skipped up the path and disappeared inside.

Mark made his way back home, opened the door and into the darkness once more!

He woke the following morning a bit worse for wear wondering whether he had dreamt the last night's events – too much whisky probably. The memory of yesterday's argument came flooding back.

He drank a hurried coffee whilst checking his diary for the day before he grabbed his briefcase and coat and made his way to the car. It was an hour's drive to work - plenty of time to rehearse an apology, he thought.

Opening the car door he tossed his briefcase inside followed by his coat. He was just about to get in when he heard a rustling sound by his feet. Looking down, out of the corner of his eye he spied a little white fluffy rabbit hopping across the grass. He grabbed his coat and launched himself at the frightened animal.

'Got ya'.

With the furry bundle struggling inside the coat, he made his way across to the cottage where he had dropped off the little girl last night. In the daylight, he could see just how pretty the cottages were.

He tapped on the door trying to restrain the struggling creature and a few minutes later the door was opened by the little girl. A familiar smell wafted passed his nose.

'As promised,' Mark said, holding out the bundle.

'You found her,' she said gleefully. From the top of the stairs came a woman's voice.

'Hello,' she called, as she strode down the stairs. 'You must be the nice man...'

As she came into view he was shocked. The oranges wafted passed his nose once again. She laughed.

'Oh Mark.'

'I brought the rabbit back,' he stuttered awkwardly. She looked good without makeup he thought.

'Thank you so much, she loves her rabbit. By the way my daughter's name is Poppy'; we moved here soon after her father left me.'

Suddenly for Mark, the day just got a whole lot brighter!

THE BAG OF MEMORIES

Shelagh O'Grady

It was a warm, sunny day but the old lady who sat on the bench overlooking the sea didn't notice that. She was clutching an old straw bag which contained mementoes of the precious moments in her life.

Putting her hand inside the bag she drew out a photo of a young man standing proudly beside a small sailing boat. Her son had loved the sea; he had sailed with his father from when he had been a small boy. One day, he and his friends had set off in the small boat of which he was so proud, intending to sail down the coast. From nowhere storm clouds had appeared and a strong wind began to blow. The little boat had capsized and all on board had perished. It had been a most terrible time in her life and she put the picture away, trying to push the sad memories to the back of her mind. Whilst in the bag her hand found the piece of string with all the fancy knots with special names that her son had given her. At Sea Scouts he had learnt to tie these knots and made her this little keepsake, but that had been a long ago.

She thought about his sister who had been a pretty, smiling baby, a happy child whose one ambition was to become a doctor. The university graduation photo showed a beaming young woman, keen to get on with her life. The old lady had felt intense pride that day. As with all young women, her daughter had soon found that special boyfriend, and before long there had been a wedding. The happy couple had decided that life would be even better on the other side of the world, and had emigrated to Australia. Eventually there were three lovely grand children. She didn`t see them very often and felt that she hardly knew them. Of course there were the letters and photos, but it was the little drawings from the grand children that she kept carefully folded in her bag. She opened a small box and gently touched the lock of golden hair which glistened in the sun, remembering her daughter`s head of curls from when she was young.

Next, she pulled a pale blue silk tie from the bag. Rubbing it gently against her cheek, she thought of her husband. They had been sweethearts at school and had married whilst they were still young. The arrival of their two beautiful children had brought them much happiness. The accident that had robbed them of their son had deeply scarred her husband and he was never the same man again. He had rarely smiled and withdrew into himself. When their daughter had moved to Australia he had gone more deeply into himself, and had passed away soon after the birth of their first grand child.

That too had been many years ago and now she lived by herself with a large tabby cat for company. The cat had been getting older and increasingly frail. One night she had tucked him into his basket and had lovingly stroked his silky fur, feeling his old bones poking through as he was getting thinner. Next morning she had found his cold furry body still curled up in his basket as she had left him the night before. As the tears began to flow she picked him up and held him gently, caressing his head and smoothing his fine bushy tail, whilst humming a little tune.

The cat`s passing had been several weeks ago and every day since she had sat on this bench with her bag of memories, and the body of her furry friend carefully placed in there too. She would gently stroke the fur and talk to him.

'There`s no one left now. The others are too far away. It will soon be my time to leave and I am quite ready to go. I pray that the good Lord will not keep me waiting too long.'

THE CHOICE OF A LIFETIME

Daniel Sams

On a cold autumn morning, out in the open fields a battle raged, two armies of six men each fought for glory and honour, whilst trying to gain control on the orb of power which lay in the field awaiting a new master.

One young man was tasked with defending his castle gate from any enemy knights. He watched on the battle with haste and anxiety as all the knights fought for orb; he stood his ground and saw as his time was upon him.

An enemy had secured the orb and began heading his way. In surety the young man lifted his shield and stood firm as the knight raced towards him, the orb giving him power and speed, but could also become a weapon against the defender. As the knight drew closer, with power unleashing from the orb, he kicked it towards the gate with such speed and velocity, the young defender was in awe and regrettably was unable to stop orb from crashing into the castle gate. Saddened the young defender sank to his knees and as he looked out to his fellow warriors, one of whom called to him.

'You are such a loser, Kevin.' the boy called out.

Kevin got up off his knees.

'I'm sorry, it was too fast for me to catch it.' he mumbled.

'Well maybe if you weren't so fat and stopped daydreaming you might be able to move quicker,' the boy continued. Kevin sunk his head as he and the rest the boys headed back to the locker rooms.

'That's the last time we let him in goal," he heard one of the boys mutter.

'That's the last time we let him on the pitch,' another replied, laughing.

After his mandatory sports lesson of the day, when break time arrived, Kevin made his way to the school library, the only place he really wanted to be anyway. He picked up his favourite fantasy book and began reading tales of heroic knights in a far-off land who were strong, agile and always requested to do the honourable thing. People held them in great esteem and men would follow them into battle without fear. Kevin wished that one day his life would be like this, but he was only thirteen years old, had long straggly hair, wore glasses and was kind of chubby, food being a great comforter which she fed whenever she could.

At school he was definitely not popular with the boys, ridiculed *for always reading, not being good enough at sports or being too* much of a teacher's pet because of his excellent test results and grades. The girls were even worse. None would look at him twice, they would avoid sitting next to him and would constantly giggle behind his back.

Back in class, after the bell had gone, their English essays they had done at the weekend, on writing, structure and grammar were being handed back, and Kevin of course had passed with flying colours and Mr Gould, the English master, took his habitual vicarious pleasure in praising him in front of everyone. Kevin cringed.

'Wonderful work as usual, Kevin,' said Mr Gould. 'I enjoyed how you discuss all the points in which you make a story worth reading; excellent work.'

'It's a shame he can't write about how to be a better football player,' the boy behind Kevin sneered.

The teacher looked at the boy.

'Now now, football is not that important in life, just because Kevin isn't very good at one thing doesn't mean he isn't better than you at everything else,' Mr Gould retorted pleasantly.

201

'We are going to get you for that, think your better than us do you?' The boy snarled quietly at Kevin when the teacher turned his back.

Later that day after school, Kevin was making his usual walk home, along a woodland path - an abandoned railway line that used to run through the town years ago. Tall trees loomed over him and he sensed a brooding, uneasy presence. He believed he was not alone.

He walked at a faster pace with mounting anxiety. He was correct there was a rustle by the side of the embankment and he turned to face the noise. His heart sank in panic as he saw the boys from his class making their way quickly towards him. He turned to flee as quickly as his chubby legs could carry him.

His flight was short; they caught up with him quickly, the boy from the classroom grabbing his arm tightly.

'I told you we were coming for you, fatty.' the boy barked.

'Please, just let me go home.' His plaintiff wail was too late, the boy punched him hard in the stomach, and then again in the face, and whilst dazed, they dragged him over to the top of the embankment, and chucked him down, laughing as Kevin slithered to the bottom.

Kevin lay there, sobbing fitfully until he heard them leave. He tried to push himself up and as he put his hand into the muddy earth, he felt something cold, hard and metallic. His fingers pried out the object and his mouth fell open with astonishment. It was a necklace, a gold collar with inscriptions on it. He placed the artifact around his neck and suddenly in a flash of light he saw visions of two future lives. One where he was the most popular boy in school, had loads of friends and girlfriends and was great at football, found a wife at a young age and had loads of kids. In the other he studied hard, passed all his GSCEs and A-levels and went on to write a fantasy novel, which in later life would go on to become a best-seller.

He called out: 'What do these mean?'

A delicate, yet clear voice echoed through the woods, booming around his brain.

'Choose your wish, Kevin.'

Kevin paused.

THE DECISION

Clare Connolly

Slouched low in her waiting-room seat, wearing that mutinous expression perfected by teenagers, Sophie examined her nails morosely, bit them, examined them more closely, bit them some more and then drummed them on the arms of the chair. Desultorily, rising to her feet, she wandered across to the magazine-strewn coffee-table, listlessly poked through its offerings, discarded them and retreated to the safety of her seat. Hiding behind a curtain of dark lank hair she lapsed into her own private world.

'Sophie Robinson,' called the receptionist. Jerked from her reverie and clutching her baggy coat closer around her, Sophie slunk across the room, trailing her feet in her scuffed fur-lined suede boots. Sitting in the consulting-room she waited.

'How can I help?' asked the doctor. Sophie, head-bowed, eyes obscured by a thick fringe, fixed her gaze on the doctor's stethoscope. Her lips moved, but no sound escaped.

'Yes?' encouraged the doctor gently. Sophie's fingers clenched and unclenched, her lips quivered and trembled but formed no recognizable words. Tears seeped from under her broody eyelashes and fell in soft splashes.

'Look at me, Sophie,' coaxed the doctor, touching her hand reassuringly. Wiping away the tears with the back of her hand, Sophie slowly raised her despairing eyes to meet those of the doctor.

'I've been a doctor for quite some time, Sophie, and I have teenage daughters of my own. I've heard it all and there's nothing you can say to shock me. Okay?'

Sophie nodded.

'Perhaps it would help if I asked you some questions,' she suggested and, taking Sophie's silence as assent, began.

'Is it something to do with sex?'

Slowly Sophie nodded, dumbly.

'Okay, I know this must be difficult for you Sophie, but do you think you might be pregnant?' The question hung, orphan-like, in the air until the almost imperceptible movement of Sophie's head confirmed the doctor's instinct.

***

The embarrassing and humiliating ordeal of the examination over, Sophie slumped into her chair again and steeled herself for the expected but dreaded diagnosis. She'd already peed on a stick and endured the two-minute eternity, willing the line to turn red. It was blue.

'Right, Sophie, you *are* pregnant. By my calculation you're about twenty-three weeks, so I guess you've known for a long time.' Sophie nodded as she continued. 'Does anyone else know about this?' Sophie shook her head.

'Twenty-three weeks. That's a long time to harbour a secret you obviously aren't happy about.'

'I was just hoping it would go away, like I'd miscarry or something,' said Sophie miserably, finally managing to find her voice.

'I see you've just turned sixteen. I expect you're worried about telling your parents.' Sophie sat silently. 'What about the father? Does he know?' enquired the doctor.

'No!' said Sophie, vehemently.

'Am I right in thinking you are here today because you want a termination, an abortion?' continued the doctor. Sophie nodded, wiping the tears from her puffy red eyes.

'Well, you'll have to decide quickly, I'm afraid. It's not legal to have an abortion beyond twenty-four weeks and it takes a few days to arrange, so you haven't got long. I suggest you tell your parents. There'll probably be skin and hair flying at first but parents are often far more supportive than you think. Once they get used to the idea they might be delighted at the prospect of being grandparents!' she said brightly.

'No, they wouldn't,' retorted Sophie with conviction.

'Well, you have a big decision to make. Ask yourself, do you want this baby? Could you love it? I hope you make the decision which is right for you. No-one else can help you with that.'

The doctor's gaze remained on the closed door for some time after Sophie's departure. She had this sort of conversation far more often than she liked. She felt sorry for these young girls, mere children really. This one was under-age when she became pregnant. It was probably the result of some binge-drinking orgy. She'd seen plenty of these 'jail-bait', as her husband called them, on Saturday nights in the town, staggering all over the place, well beyond the use of reason. She probably didn't even know who the father was! Mind you, this one didn't seem the type, a bit dowdy and unkempt. Still, it was often the quiet ones.

Armed with the leaflets the doctor had given her, a devastated Sophie left the surgery feeling the eyes of the waiting patients boring into her soul, judging her. Walking swiftly but aimlessly, she found herself on the tow-path by the canal. Wearily, she sank on a bench and stared into the fast-flowing murky waters, mesmerised by the patterns of the currents around and over the rocks and outcrops. Her head swirled fit to bursting, bombarded by a thousand thoughts and torments. She forced herself to focus on the most pressing and tried to visualize telling her parents, experimenting with words which might convey how this situation had occurred. She would need to tell them *everything*. But, it was unimaginable. The fall-out would wrench her world asunder. She knew from experience her mother would be no help. That grim thought tortured and angered her. This would be the end of family life as she knew it. She would have to leave home. Where would she go?

The doctor's question reverberated in her head, 'Do you want this baby?' Well, she *would* love a baby, if truth be told, something of her own to love and care for. She had excelled in her Childcare classes at school and had already signed-up for an NVQ in Childcare when she left school. She would be a good mother. But did she want **this** baby? Did she want a reminder-made-flesh of its father? Suddenly, her life-shattering way became clear. One hand shuffled through the leaflets, the other produced her mobile. Trembling fingers dialled the number.

'Hello, is that Childline? I'd like to talk to someone about sexual abuse…my Dad,' she wept.

THE DOMINO EFFECT

Della Millward

Kay was on her way to get the weekly shop when she heard the travel news.

'Reports are coming in of a multi car traffic accident near junction 4 of the M3. Stay tuned to Urban City Views – the station that keeps you up to date.'

She felt a flicker of worry because Rob was on his way to Heathrow Airport. The chance of him being involved was small, she knew, but all the same she pulled into the next lay by and rang him on his mobile.

No answer – and he had hands-free so she knew he'd answer if he could. There was no need to worry, but she did worry.

As she was sitting there, the cheery voice of the traffic reporter broke into her uneasy thoughts.

'The M3 is now closed between junctions 3 and 5. Long delays are expected. Avoid the area like *The Plague*.' There was a half laughing shudder in his voice.

At the supermarket Kay tried Rob's mobile again. Then she texted him in case he'd stopped for a comfort break. Yes, that was where he'd be, sitting in a motorway services, reading the paper, oblivious. He was always too early for airport pick ups; he left plenty of time for all eventualities. Careful, cautious Rob. He never broke the speed limit on motorways either.

'Driving bumper to bumper is what causes most motorway pile ups,' he'd said once when she was worried about the amount of time he spent on the road. 'It's called the domino effect. The first car makes a mistake and the rest of them are too close to avoid the consequences. So they all get caught up in the chaos.'

There was no reason to think Rob was involved. Except, of course, it

212

was about the right time for him to be close and he wasn't answering his phone. It had been fifteen minutes since she'd first tried it.

Fear, which until now, she'd kept firmly suppressed beneath her sensible wife facade, began to coil up inside her like smoke. It caught at her breath. What if he wasn't answering his phone because he was trapped inside his car which was now a twisted lump of metal on its roof?

Please keep him safe? She said the words in her head, but they were more of a shout than a quiet prayer.

What if it was too late for praying and he was already dead? A great black hole left in a world where his presence was her raison d'être.

Stop it! she told herself. Stop thinking like that. It wasn't helpful. Her hands were now sweaty on her phone which lay silent in her lap. People walked past her car: two girls swinging Hessian shopping bags, laughing and joking; a family with a small boy clutching his father's hand. She could smell the vanilla air freshener in the overheated space. She opened the window and let in a faint mix of diesel fumes as someone parked a 4x4 behind her.

And then a text came through. Two words. *I'm fine.* The relief washed through her cooler than a sea breeze in a desert. She felt faint with it. Hot, cold, sweaty. Everything was sharper, more beautiful; the sun on the tarmac outside; the smile on an old man's face as he turned to his wife.

She dialled Rob's number, and this time he answered instantly.

'Sorry, I didn't hear the phone. Bit of trouble on the motorway.' His voice sounded shaky.

'But you're OK. You're not involved?'

'I'm fine. I'm sort of in the middle of it. Tell you later. Could you phone the airport? Get them to tell my client I'm running late.'

* * *

Much later, at home on their sofa, in the snugness of Saturday night normality he told her about the car that had hit the central reservation and spun, about the domino effect of other cars not able to stop, metal smashing into metal. How he'd been on the outskirts, in the middle lane, how he'd managed to brake just before the carnage.

'I saw a man running away from his car. It was on fire and an old woman was trapped inside. And he just ran and ran.'

'What happened?' she asked, shock flattening her voice as she looked at his stricken face.

'I was trying to get there, I was running towards it, but I was too late. The car exploded. A fireball of metal. And that man, Kay, he never even looked back.'

'He must have been terribly afraid.' She wanted to take the pictures out of his head.

'A coward," he said. 'He left her to die.'

'A human,' she said, 'struggling to survive.'

'Yeah, with humans like that, I wonder if there's any hope for mankind.' He sighed. 'There was this old geezer. The kind you wouldn't notice ordinarily, he had a long grey ponytail. Anyway, I helped him get some kiddies out a car. The doors were stoved in so he passed them out the windscreen.'

'Were they okay?'

'Yeah, mainly thanks to him. He was really calm. A bit later I saw him with this woman. She was trapped under her car and he just lay beside her – he lay in a pool of petrol, holding her hand.'

He buried his head in her shoulder and she stroked his hair.

'It was a nightmare, Kay, my worst nightmare.'

'It's over now.' She knew the pictures in his head would never be over. He'd always see that man running away, that car exploding. She would have to keep reminding him the guy with the ponytail had been doing something amazing. As long as there were people like him around, mankind had a great future.

Rob would come to see that too, in time, because that was how it worked. One tiny act of kindness led to another, which led to another and then another – that was the domino effect of love.

THE FARE

S. J. Scally

Twenty eight, thirty, there! That must be it. I pull up at the kerb and toot my horn then gaze out of the window for a second until I see the curtain twitch. I know the routine. First they check it's for them then they take a few seconds to get their coats and bags before rushing out.

'Control, this is Jack. I'm at thirty two Coronation Road.'

'Roger that Jack. Let me know when you've dropped off.' I turn the volume down on the radio, as the sound of a front door slamming makes me look up. Running away from the little terraced house is a blonde. She's dressed in a long grey military-type coat which seems to make her look small, long black boots cover her legs. She looks like a member of the red army and I didn't even think it had been that cold this Christmas.

'Hello there,' she says in a quiet, posh accent and the taxi fills with a beautiful floral aroma as she climbs in the back. I turn to look at her. She's about my age and really pretty. At first it doesn't look like she's wearing any make up but as I look closer I can see it; well applied to make her look natural. Very different to Gemma's make up which was always slapped on like grease paint. We used to argue about it. I didn't see why she had to wear make up really and I certainly didn't like kissing her through a layer of gunk. Well, I don't have to worry about that now, do I? In fact, I'm surprised. I haven't thought about her for ages, which I suppose is a good sign isn't it? I realise I'm staring at my passenger.

'Hello,' I say, trying to make a good impression. 'You're well wrapped up.' And she smiles at me. It's a nice smile. She's got nice straight teeth and she looks right into my eyes. 'Where are we off to then?'

'Morrisons, please.' She settles back in her seat and looks out the window. 'Getting cold out there, isn't it?'

I nod and pull out into the road. There isn't much traffic around and in no time we've left the little lane behind and we're heading towards the town.

'So, have you run out of turkey already?' I glance in my mirror and catch her eye. She smiles shyly at me and my stomach does a little flip. For a second we seem to make a connection.

'Actually, I should've been away still but well, my plans changed.' Her voice tails off and there's silence, except for the indicator ticking. 'Broke up with my boyfriend,' she offers quietly, volunteering the information as we pull out of the junction.

'Oh, I'm sorry.'

'Don't be,' she leans forwards, closer to my seat. 'He was a manipulative bully and I'm well rid.'

'Oh.' I don't really know what to say, so I don't say anything else. I concentrate on the road, check my mirrors and fiddle with the heating dial and eventually she slumps back in her seat and sighs.

'That sounded horrible, didn't it?' I can feel her watching me in the mirror and as I glance at it she looks sad. 'He wasn't that bad, we just weren't good for each other. Nobodies fault.'

'Tough, though isn't it?' I nod, fully able to sympathise with her. 'I broke up with my girlfriend a few months ago – well, I say I, but it was her who finished it.'

'Oh, dear. Sorry, didn't mean to drag up old memories.' She sounds suddenly wretched and I feel as if that's my fault.

'Oh I'm fine now,' I add hastily.

'Are you over her now then?'

'Yeah, we're still friends.'

'Well, you can't force it can you?' she said. 'If it's meant to be it's meant to be as my mum used to say.'

By now we've reached Morrisons and I pull into the dropping off bay. Without waiting for me to say anything, she fishes about in her purse for some cash and hands me a fiver.

'Keep the change.'

As I turn to thank her she sticks her hand out towards me and waits for me to shake it.

'I'm Phil. It was nice to meet you, er...'

'Oh, I'm Jack.'

I beam my biggest smile and pump her hand up and down before reluctantly releasing it. Her hand feels small and soft and only seems to highlight the size of my great paw.

'Well, nice to meet you, Jack. Hope you have a great new year.'

And with that she hops out, giving me a little wave before disappearing into the supermarket.

THE FOOTBALL MATCH

Ruth Hughes

It was a Saturday morning in March, Jamie and his father were getting ready to go to watch Arsenal v Liverpool at the Emirates Stadium in London.

'Dad, what time are we leaving?' asked Jamie.

'We will be leaving in about an hour, so you need to finish your breakfast, clean your teeth and get ready,' he replied.

'What are we doing for lunch? Can we go to McDonalds?'

'I'll see; it depends how good you are.'

Jamie finished his meal quickly and did everything he was asked. He was ready to go. They got some snacks for their journey, said goodbye and got in the car, and drove off.

On the way they listened to the party dance CD from where they go on holiday. They were singing Y.M.C.A. at the top of their voices, Jamie doing the dance while passers-by laughed at them.

It took them about an hour and a half to get to the Emirates. When they got there they went to get some lunch. They then took a slow walk back to the Emirates, heading for the gate where they had to go in. When they were allowed to enter the stadium they went and got a drink, and made their way to their seats. Jamie's mother had managed to get front row tickets for them; they could see the whole pitch at the same level as the players. Behind the goals were Theo Walcott and Thierry Henry warming up for Arsenal at one end, and at the other, Andy Carroll and Jamie Carragher warming up for Liverpool. Jamie managed to get their autographs as they came off the pitch to go and get ready for the match.

At 2:45 all the players from both teams came out onto the pitch ready to start at 3 o'clock. Jamie became increasingly excited as the seconds

222

passed so slowly towards kick off time.

All the players shook hands with each other, the captains tossed a coin to decide who would kick off first and their team flags were swapped. Arsenal won the toss and the captain decided to kick off. Within five minutes the score was 1 – 0 to Arsenal; it carried on like that for about ten minutes when Steven Gerrard scored for Liverpool and made the 1-1; it was still the same score at half time.

'Dad, can a have a hotdog please?' asked Jamie.

'I can't believe you are still hungry after what you ate for lunch.'

'I am a growing lad.'

'Okay , I'll go and get you one.' So his dad went off to the kiosk to get a hotdog for Jamie.

When he got back Jamie was missing, his dad started to get worried when he heard a voice ask, 'What's your name, son?'

'My name is Jamie and I'm here with my dad, John. Hi, dad!' he said, waving.

His father turned round to see Jamie standing in the middle of the pitch. A red track-suited man, a football tucked under one arm, the other round Jamie's shoulder, was walking Jamie towards the goal area.

'Right, Jamie,' he said. 'All you have to do is take a penalty and score to win the prize. Do you think you can do that?'

'I hope so.' Jamie put the ball on the penalty spot and looked up at the goalkeeper. Drawing a deep breath he took a few steps back before running towards the ball. His kick was clean and hard, the ball smacking against the netting behind the 'keeper's desperate dive. Jamie performed a celebratory circuit of the pitch to the applause of a delighted crowd.

'Well done, Jamie,' said the man. 'Your prize is a season ticket for next season and a day of training with the Arsenal team. Is that okay for you, Jamie?'

'Yes, that's great. Thank you, it is going to be the best day of my life.'

'Well done again Jamie, you can go back to your dad now.'

'Thank you.' Jamie walked back to his dad.

'Dad, did you hear that?'

'Yes it's brilliant, your mother will be so happy.'

Jamie ate his hotdog whilst they waited for the second half to commence. Liverpool kicked off and about ten minutes into the second half someone ran onto the pitch and hit Luis Suarez in the face, which enlivened the crowd. It took the police five minutes to get this person off the pitch. When the match restarted Liverpool scored within two minutes, but Arsenal evened the score five minutes later.

About two minutes before the end of the match Arsenal scored again. The final score was 3-2 to Arsenal, a result that made father and son very happy.

They left the stadium and made their way back to the car. Jamie immediately phoned his mum to let her know they were on the way home. By the time they arrived Jamie had fallen asleep, dreaming of scoring a Cup Final penalty for Arsenal at Wembley.

Bursting with excitement and pride he couldn't wait to tell his mother all about it.

'Mum, I scored the half-time goal and I have won a season ticket for next year and a training day with the Arsenal squad.'

'Your joking, Jamie!' said his mother.

'No, mum. It's true!' he said. 'What a wonderful day I've had! But I'll tell you all about it in the morning. I'm going to bed now.' Jamie yawned expansively as he was about to leave the room, but stopped, turned to his mother and said, 'Oh, by the way mum, thanks for getting us those seats. If it weren't for you I wouldn't have been near enough to the pitch to be picked out for the half-time penalty.'

He gave her a kiss and went to bed.

***

When Jamie awoke the next day, he pinched himself black and blue before he could accept that he had not been dreaming.

THE JOURNEY

Mary Coward

The wind tore relentlessly through their clothes as the group of people stumbled along the rough path trying to protect their eyes from the coarse dust which was whipping across their faces.

There were several families with children of various ages, many crying as they were being helped along. Only the babies, wrapped securely on their mothers' backs, travelled in comfort. Their tiny faces were relaxed and sleepy, as they were lulled by the movement and warmth of their mothers.

These gentle people were used to a hard way of life in a remote area. They looked forward to the rare occasions that brought colour and happiness to their lives. They had risen early in the pale dawn and had quietly prepared for the long journey.

The women and young girls had busied themselves around crackling fires making a breakfast of warm dough. Some was carefully wrapped in cloth bundles for the journey beside their filled water containers. The young boys were feeding the animals and helping the men to get ready; there was an atmosphere of quiet excitement among them.

A few elderly people among the group watched as the preparations were made. They were unable to travel to the distant village in the valley, but they remembered other times, when they had been young, strong and the vibrant members of the group - the sound of the music, singing and dancing of those days lingered mistily in their minds, a gentle glow within them of past happiness and a wish that the young people would enjoy similar experiences.

When the preparations had been completed, the villagers gathered the gifts that they had lovingly made: Wood carvings and richly coloured materials were packed with care. There were also fruits and little baskets filled with shiny, dark nuts which the children had gathered. Then the moment came for their departure. They turned to wave to those left behind, the sounds of their good wishes following them. A playful breeze tugged at their loose garments appearing to pull them towards their destination.

Their excitement was hard to contain as they began to climb the bare hills that surrounded their village. The sun was warm and lit up the contours of their ebony features. They strode purposefully along a high ridge that would lead them into a deep valley. After an hour or so, they were aware that the wind had greatly increased...a storm was approaching. As they continued, it became more and more difficult to keep together as a group, but they encouraged one another and slowly made their way through the barren landscape.

Later the sun became obscured by menacing dark clouds and rain began to beat heavily on their exposed faces and limbs. They were forced to take shelter between huge rocks that littered the way, but they were hungry and welcomed the chance to eat and rest. The food bundles were shared eagerly and the cool water soon quenched their parched throats. The babies snuggled hungrily at their mothers breasts, their trusting eyes fixed steadfastly on the tender faces above them.

Afterwards, the children began to scramble over the rocks searching for lizards and insects, while the adults discussed the progress of their journey. It was taking longer than they had planned. Some were worried that they'd taken a wrong path during the storm but the leaders remained strong in their belief that they were going in the right direction. They reached agreement and made ready to continue.

The rain had stopped, but the wind still tore at their bodies. Clouds were scudding rapidly across the dark sky as patches of sunlight struggled to break through. The villagers were walking at a good pace again towards the welcome that awaited them and this thought helped them to face the biting wind.

One of the young women had a special reason for wanting to reach the distant village. She was to meet the family of a boy who wanted to marry her. She was apprehensive, but also excited and because of her happiness almost unaware of being wet and cold.

After her the marriage she would leave her home. This thought saddened her, but she loved the boy and his gentle eyes had declared his love. They had first met as children, but during the past year they had spoken of their love. She was longing to see him and the road seemed easier, as her thoughts led her towards her new life.

The villagers moved down the hillside in a ripple of colour, the golden grasses blending, bending with their bodies in supple, rhythmic movements. Suddenly there was a shrill cry from a young boy who had fallen into a gully suffering a jagged gash across his forehead. The people ahead halted; the boy's father lifted him on to a flat patch of parched earth to tend to his wound. A young girl ran to them and uttered soothing words as she dampened a piece of cloth. The boy's eyes grew large and watery as she gently bathed the wound, but he was bravely silent. His broad strong father comforted him and bound his son's head with a strip of cloth from his own clothing, before lifting him into his arms to carry him for the rest of the journey.

As they continued, the sky lightened; they knew that they were almost there; a ripple of joy ran through them. They soon broke into a traditional chant to express their elation and their music carried clearly across the now open valley. Suddenly the travellers were aware of voices in the distance and through the haze of dust and sunlight they were able to make out the indistinct shapes of people. The figures drew nearer, and then they were upon them, strong arms lifting the exhausted children, speaking in soft tones to them. The adults embraced each other, their dark skins and the rich colours of their clothing merging into brilliant patterns of warmth. They had arrived.

THE RIVERSIDE TEAROOMS

Irene Burnett-Thomas

Miriam was mystified about the butter. She was certain she had put a dish on each table. She wasn't going senile just yet.

'Ellie, sort the tables out, please dear. Tables six and seven haven't got any butter, and table five's got three dishes!'

'OK, Miriam, won't take a minute,' said Ellie cheerfully. Ellie had grown fond of Miriam and hated to see her worried about anything.

The Riverside Tearooms in Washbourne, an attractive market town on the south coast, were doing well since Miriam and her husband Reg opened last summer, with young Ellie and Sophie as waitresses.

'All sorted,' called Ellie. 'Everything's perfect now.'

Miriam decided to close the windows at the front of the cafe to keep it cosy on the early spring day. She glanced out at the twin towers of Washbourne Minster church, with their beautiful grey stonework against the blue sky. She looked around to admire the pretty pink and white colour scheme of the cafe.

The first people arrived around ten o'clock. Some ordered fruit scones with jam, others cheese scones with butter.

'Delicious', said one.

'The best scones ever,' complimented another.

Just before eleven, in bounced Sophie, hair flowing behind her. She hurried to the staff-room to change into her black dress and frilly white apron. She tucked her hair into the cap. Miriam liked the girls to be dressed this way - quintessentially English and a little old-fashioned. Sophie had moaned at first, but soon got used to the outfit, as she wanted to go to catering college, and the job would look good on her C.V.

232

'Bit chilly in here, felt quite a draught,' said Sophie under her breath, as she emerged.

'Don't be silly, all the windows are shut,' said Ellie.

'Come now, girls, let's get on,' encouraged Miriam. 'It's going to get busy soon.'

The day turned out to be a good one, with visitors from all over the country, and even a couple from the States 'doing the south-west of England', who ordered a cream-tea with two scones each. A charming French family came in and enjoyed an English afternoon tea of cucumber sandwiches and lemon drizzle cake.

At half past six, Miriam shut up shop. She closed the chintz curtains in the front and turned the key in the lock, looking forward to an evening at home with Reg. This was their last venture before retirement, and Miriam was tired by the end of the day.

The following morning Miriam was back to open up. That's very strange, she thought to herself. One curtain was pulled back. Ellie must have got here early today. After all she had trusted her with her own key, just in case. Miriam entered the cafe and looked around.

'You there, Ellie?'

But there was no reply. She went through to the kitchen and the staff-room. There was no-one else there. Miriam found it hard to concentrate on setting up for the day, worrying about the curtains and losing her mind.

When Ellie and Sophie had both arrived, Miriam told them what had happened.

'Oh Miriam, you must have forgotten to close them properly,' suggested

Sophie.

'Try not to worry so much,' said Ellie kindly.

But Miriam knew she had closed the curtains, as she did religiously every night.

It was spitting with rain most of the day, and the Riverside Tearooms were not quite as busy as usual. A few customers came in with umbrellas and macks dripping, glad to be in the warm and order a 'nice pot of tea'.

'Ellie, would you collect up all the salt and pepper pots, please?' asked Miriam, when they were out of ear-shot of the customers. 'I want to give them a good clean before I go tonight.' She ran a bowl of piping hot water and detergent and began to wipe the little pots. She left them on the table in the kitchen to dry overnight.

Usually weekends were the busiest at the Riverside Tearooms. People came to look round the individual shops in Washbourne, searching for something unusual to wear in the boutiques, for quirky shoes in Lauren and Lily, or for a new gadget from the impressive kitchen shop. Then they wanted refreshment.

Miriam opened up on Saturday morning. The first thing she saw was a salt and pepper pot on table one. Either I really am going mad, or Ellie must be in before me this time, she thought.

'Hello there,' she called. No answer.

The other salt and pepper pots were where she had left them, neatly lined up in the kitchen. When Ellie arrived, Miriam asked her to put them out on the tables.

'Ellie, I'm worried,' she said. 'Table one had salt and pepper when I

234

came in.'

'That's impossible,' replied Ellie. 'I removed them all yesterday.'

'I know you did, dear.'

'Must be a ghost,' joked Ellie, trying to lighten things a little. But Miriam could not laugh with her. Ellie noticed her anxious face and said,

'Everyone makes mistakes and forgets things sometimes.'

Miriam and the girls were thinking about clearing up after another busy day, when a couple came in, asking for tea and Victoria sponge cake.

'Sophie, go see if there's any sponge left, please. There might be only fruit cake, or the last piece of date and walnut,' said Miriam.

While Sophie was away, the elderly lady talked in a loud voice, as her gentleman companion appeared to be deaf. He leant towards her, eager for her gossip.

'Of course this is the cafe that old Mrs. Danvers lived above. She hated all the banging and crashing of the pots and pans and the laughter of families in the summer. Bitter and resentful she was, face all pinched. Dead now, the old dear.'

Miriam's ears pricked up. Maybe that explains it all, she thought. If you believe in ghosts, that is!

THE ROMANCE

Bob Hitching

Peter and Paula met, as many young couples do today, at the local disco. It was not a case of immediate attraction on either side but their feelings gradually grew stronger the longer they knew each other. They made a lovely couple, as both sets of parents agreed.

At first, they met only on Fridays at the disco, but soon Peter asked her out increasingly frequently. Paula was impressed by his gallantry and thoughtfulness, quite unlike those boys she had dated before. He never complained when she was late – one of Paul's few failings. In all other aspects of his behaviour (which needn't be examined here!) Peter was always the perfect gentleman.

On her part, Paula was also most considerate and unselfish. Eventually, after four or five months, she didn't think of going out with anyone else – and neither did Peter.

From early on, she romantically hoped that one day he would pop the question and even than she knew what her reply would be. It may seem strange in these modern times for an old-fashioned "Mills and Boon" romance to flourish, but it did.

Peter always bought her flowers on Fridays.

'We met on a Friday, my love,' he would remind her every time. Not that she needed reminding!

When they very occasionally ate out, she was always careful never to order the expensive dishes, and there was never a question of their going Dutch. Although he was only a junior manager, he was confident (and so was she) that he was on the way up. But, to be honest, as a dental receptionist, Paula probably took home nearly as much as he did.

Although she did not like watching football at all, she would join him on the terraces at Selhurst Park on the occasional Saturday afternoon.

Similarly, Peter would patiently sit through the silly-to-him romantic movies she most enjoyed, as he did at the Odeon on one particular Sunday...

All evening he seemed on edge, if not rather nervous and was unusually quiet on the walk home through the park. When they stopped and sat on their usual seat, watching the ducks in the gathering gloom, Peter gently took her hand and, not entirely to her surprise, stammered out the question, 'Will you marry me, Paula?' He quickly added, 'but perhaps you'd like some time to think about it?'

Without hesitation she replied after kissing him tenderly.

'Yes, of course I will, Peter.'

He smiled broadly and produced an exquisite turquoise ring from his pocket – where he had been touching it all evening – and slipped it onto her third finger. It fitted perfectly and looked just right. Paula couldn't take her eyes off it.

He then suggested which he had never done before, that they go back to his place and perhaps watch a video there. She agreed and as they were walking slowly, hand-in-hand planning their future together, for no apparent reason, out of the blue, he suggested that they could sit together on his huge sofa in front of the fire at the flat and maybe have some of his favourite snack: Marmite and toast.

At this, Paula stiffened, quickly released her hand from his and drew away. Slowly, she took the beautiful ring from her finger and gave it back to him. Sobbing, and through copious tears she said:

'I do love you very much, darling but I am so sorry I could never live with a man who likes Marmite. It's all off.'

And regretfully, so very regretfully, as she walked away from him, Paula whispered, 'Goodbye, Peter, goodbye, my love.'

UNCOMFY

Bob Hitching

The very first time we went to look at the house, the front door seemed to be stuck and we really had to push our way in. And it was always that way. No problem ever to go out through it, but it needed a bit of a shove to open from the outside. Not only I, but also various visitors had a look at it. But none of us were able to see why this should be.

However, when we got inside we fell in love with the place - nice atmosphere, we felt - and we moved in within a month.

The twins Susan and Peter (seven years old) soon made themselves at home and we all settled in nicely.

Funny thing, though: none of us ever seemed to argue when we were indoors. The kids would fight outside in the garden, as they always had, but changed as soon as they got inside. No squabbling. Same with Betty and me; we had our differences, of course - always had had over the years, probably more than most - but when we were in the house, we were both willing to give way. Seemed too good to be true! Almost unnatural, it was. We both commented on it.

We noticed it with our visitors, too. For instance, my dear parents were always criticising each other and bickering at their own home and other places, but here they both went out of their way to compromise - to be honest, it was almost uncanny.

I know it sounds ridiculous, but Tigger, our cat, and Toby, the dog, scrapped as usual in the garden, but inside, they - somewhat reluctantly, it seemed to us - definitely tolerated each other. And unusually for them, they were both keen to spend as much time outdoors as possible, we certainly noticed.

We should all - humans and animals alike - have been really happy in this house but, for some reason, it was a bit of a relief to Betty and myself when I was promoted and we had to move up north.

When we told the kids they seemed to take it okay, but when I pushed them and asked why, Susan said, 'This isn't like our old house. I feel a bit uncomfy here.' Feminine intuition at seven years old! Mind you, this was the girl who told us, when she was really little, 'I can smell snow coming' and the very next morning when we woke up, there it was.

Simon was the one who, at a very early age - two maybe - tended to push my mum away when she got over-affectionate, cuddling and kissing him. So I wasn't really surprised when he nodded in agreement, 'A bit uncomfy, yes.'

We sold up remarkably quickly and when we were all packed up and ready to go, I moved to lock the door, but Betty opened it again - needing the strong push as usual!

She called out into the empty house. 'You have won, House. There is more than one way of skinning a cat, as my granny used to say. Goodbye.' As she shut the door again, we heard a definite peal of laughter echoing within.

We looked at each other and said simultaneously, 'Uncomfy.'

WALKING BACK TO HAPPINESS

Jenny Piercy

6.00am

They drove up the motorway, Anna's apprehension growing the nearer they got to Derbyshire, James's favourite area for walking.

'Penny for them,' said Julie.

'Just remembering,' said Anna.

'You'll be fine,' said Julie. 'Walking will blow the cobwebs away.'

Was she right? They started a familiar walk and Anna grew more tense the further they went. At the summit, looking across the valleys, she started to cry. She hadn't cried like this since James died. Julie hugged her and they wept together. When they stopped they were embarrassed and pulling apart, started to laugh.

'I feel better for that,' said Julie.

'Surprisingly, I think I do too,' said Anna.

'I said we'd call in on John and his Mum, do you feel up to it?'

'Yes, it would be good to catch up,' said Anna.

4.00pm A Knocking on the door.

'Come away in,' said John. 'Kettle's on.'

They followed him into the farmhouse kitchen. The table was laid for tea.

'Don't get much company since Mum died.' he said.

'We're so sorry, we didn't know,' said Julie. Anna, unable to reply, began to cry again.

'Six months since,' he said. 'Sit you down and help yourselves.'

'I can feel for you,' said Anna. 'I lost James last year.' She got up and hugged him tight.

'I hope you don't mind. Being held is the thing I've missed most.' Anna said.

'It's just what I needed.' he replied.

The awkwardness over, they caught up with village news.

'I'll miss the farm when I sell it,' he said.

The two women choked on their tea in surprise.

'You can't sell up, what would you do?' said Julie.

'I can't make a living now Mum's gone. She did some B&B and lots of other bits that made the farm viable. I can't afford to take anyone on and the lasses around here aren't interested in being a farmer's wife.'

10.50pm Last orders

At the pub, over their meal, the conversation always came back to John and the farm. Anna realised that for the first time since James's death she had thought about someone else's problems instead of her own. She didn't sleep well that night as ideas chased around her head; she'd have to run her idea past Julie tomorrow.

Saturday morning

'*Buy* the farm and make a living out of walking holidays?' said Julie.

'Can you afford it? What will happen to John?'

'I'm hoping he will stay on at the farm, keep the sheep, the land will want managing.' 'You had a high power job before, this seems a drastic change. Besides, you've never lived in the country. You can't equate a bit of camping with what it's like on a permanent basis.'

'I'm just thinking it would be a new start. Up to now nobody's wanted to employ me. I was lucky to get redundancy after James died, I was such a mess.'

'Why not just get another job in London? said Julie. 'You've got contacts and you're more together now.'

'I don't want someone looking over my shoulder all the time. I need to have my own plans.

'My flat feels like a prison, but I can't leave it because it contains all the happiness I've known. I need to sell up and break out and this could be the way,' said Anna. 'Well, think about it carefully. You can't raise John's hopes and then walk away. That's of course, if he's interested in your idea.'

Saturday 4pm

'You sure a soft southern lassie can survive the winters up here?' said John.

'There's only one way to find out,' Anna said.

They had discussed ideas and checked out the farm buildings and nearby fields. John was sceptical at first but Anna's stream of ideas enthused him with possibilities. A decision was made. Anna would sell her flat and buy into the farm; they would put in for planning permission and a Rural Development Grant.

'Good job we're not in the National Park, that'd be a real bugger,' said John.

Three Months later

It had been a strange experience living in the house together, both bereaved, not knowing each other. At first, they had kept very much to their own areas only meeting occasionally for meals. The hardest winter for decades changed that. They found themselves taking refuge in the warm kitchen and getting to talk properly for the first time.
The villagers were behind the project but were really intrigued as to what went on 'up at t'farm'; were they an item? The celebratory meals at the pub, when the planning permission and grant came through, really caused the tongues to wag.

Spring

The building work forged ahead and Anna had taken her first bookings for Easter. Family and 'walking friends' had helped out with the promise of free holidays later. John had been amazing in the number of hours he'd put in, he so wanted it to happen. Work would start again after Easter, ready for the summer.

Easter

'Still reckon you're going to make your fortune?' John teased.

'Just the first million tomorrow,' she countered.

'Come up the hill,' he said. 'You need a break.'

They walked to the old stile where they usually rested. A new bench was now in the ideal place. Anna cried as she read the engraved plate:

For James and Mum, who also loved this view.

John held her. 'You've worked real hard on this project,' he said. 'I thought you might like this.'

'Thank you. It's wonderful,' she said. 'And you've been wonderful too.'

They sat on the bench for a while in silence, then for the first time, hand in hand, they walked down the hill together.

WOMEN

Bob Hitching

He couldn't help chuckling as he came in through the front door, went out again, re-entering through the side door and then the same with the back door, trailing mud each time all over the carpets. Thinking what she'd say:

(Typical - you're useless in the garden after all these years, but still expect me to clear up after you when you come in.)

In the kitchen, the washing-up was left from last night.

(Do you think it's going to do itself?)

But he did wet a few plates and saucers and put them away without drying them.

(Don't you ever dry up properly? Why do I have to do them again every morning before I can even have breakfast?)

Tea towel thrown on the floor, of course. Pedal-bin overflowing. All cupboards and drawers left wide open.

(I don't know why I let you into my kitchen.)

He took up her early-morning cup of tea. Spilling even more than usual.

(In the saucer again! Do you think I'm a cat?)

In the toilet, he left the empty roll.
(Left to me, again.)

Then went very noisily downstairs.

(Can't you learn to be quiet?)

Took his breakfast into the lounge, where he dropped crumbs

onto the carpet and spilled coffee all over the settee.

(Worse than a two-year old, you messy thing!)

He put the crocks into the sink, making sure he chipped a plate and broke the handle off his breakfast mug.

(How careless can a grown man be?)

Going back into the lounge - slamming the door of course.

(Whatever are you doing down there?)

He proceeded to scatter newspapers and books all over every available surface.

(How many times have I told you?)

Back upstairs in the bathroom, he made sure the shower was left scummy and the hand-basin more traces of his tooth-cleaning.

(Disgusting! That's the only word for you!)

Towels left on the floor, alongside his toenail clippings.

(You know how I hate that kind of thing!)

He then dressed, taking stuff out of his wardrobe and throwing it onto the floor.

(What are you playing at today? You're even worse than usual!)

Then out into the garage, where he proceeded to warm up the car - on full throttle, naturally.

(Even if you have no consideration for me, think of the neighbours - and don't forget, it's me that has to put up with them.)

He noisily back the car out of the garage and parked it neatly just on the new flower border.

(You blind? After over forty years' driving!)

A few more revs for luck and he went back indoors, leaving the front door open.

(Are you mad? Anyone could just walk in.)

After a final look round downstairs, he went noisily back up and, leaving his shoes on, stretched out on his bed.

(I suppose Lazybones is going to lie there all day?)

Smiling, he closed his eyes and waited for her to find everything.

Sure enough, she soon came storming in.

(What did your last slave die of?)

But then, the unexpected; she started laughing and couldn't stop. Then, poking him in the ribs, between giggles, she managed to get out the words:

'OK - you win today. Now get up, move the car and help me get tidied up.'

He replied with the only thing he could say:

'*Women*!'

AUTHORS UNDER 18 YEARS

THERE'S A WOLF IN OUR OVEN

Eloise Orchard
Age 11

The toast flew out of the toaster, landing on Puffles the cat.

'Oh, sorry, Puff!' the energetic old lady apologised, scraping the bits of bread off Puffles.

Then she popped the dry pieces in her mouth, when the phone rang. She ran to fetch it, and answered, saying,

'Hello? It's little old lady Doris speaking!' A muffled squeak came from the other end. It was the first little pig.

'Hi, it's the three little pigs! Could you do us a favour please? We only eat fruit pies, and the big bad wolf is hiding in our oven so we can't bake one!' the first little pig explained, sadly.

'Go on,' urged the lady.

'Also, Wolf turned veggie - but he still hates apples. Could you be so kind as to offer us tea? But no plum pie; it's the only fruit Wolf likes and he would eat it,' the second little pig sighed.

'Oh, ok, but I only have plums. Come tonight at six o'clock. I should have swapped my plums for apples by then.' The old lady replied, before grabbing her coat to set off to swap her plums.
A little later, the little woman saw the gingerbread man, carrying a platter of smoothies.

'Hello, why are you out with those drinks, my biscuity friend?' she asked, picking one of his fingers off and cramming it in her mouth. The gingerbread man looked annoyed, but he put it behind him in order to be sweet and sell some smoothies.

'Haven't you heard? We're competing with Greggs down the road, to see who can sell the most drinks in a week, and if I don't sell some I'll be on sale in the bakery where I work!' the biscuit replied.

'I'll buy some off you! Shall we say I'll pay not with money, but – with plums?' the old lady asked.

'Plums?' asked the gingerbread man, raising one eyebrow uncertainly.

'Yes my friend, plums. It will help you get rid of some of those terrible drinks, so you won't be on sale as a crunchy, chewy, mouth-watering cookie, and...'

'Done!' cried her edible friend. Then he handed her the smoothies and danced off.

Doris was nearly at the market when she saw Jasmine, Aladdin and Aboo, the monkey. Jasmine noticed the frantic look on the little old woman's wrinkly face.

'You must be thirsty with all those drinks!' Jasmine remarked, stopping and causing Aladdin and Aboo to stop too.

'No, I don't need these, I'm just looking for something good to swap them with!' the woman said.

'And they're freshly made, full of goodness!' she added quickly.

'Smoothies! Just what we want! Aboo here is a bit bored of water, aren't you Aboo?' Aladdin spoke up.

'Ok, but what do you want in return? You can have my old pearls if you want, Aladdin is about to buy me some new ones from that new market across the street!' Jasmine preened, handing the lady a pearl bracelet.

'Why, thanks! You can have these smoothies - it's the least I can do for you.' the lady assured Jasmine. Then little old Doris strolled on, determined to find apples for her piggy friends.

259

The old woman had just reached the market, when a voice from behind her sounded.

'Oh, my hair!' The little old woman turned slowly to find Rapunzel, sobbing whilst running worried fingers through her immensely long hair.

'What's wrong?' Doris asked.

'My hair is so wet, and I can't possibly leave it till I get home; it goes all heavy and curly if I don't dry it right away.' Rapunzel whined.

'Yes, dear, but why is your hair wet?' The little old woman asked, sympathetically.

'I just won the apple bobbing world championships, and I had to dunk my head in a bowl of water at least twenty times.' Rapunzel replied.

'Hang on a tick, did you just say *apple bobbing*?' asked the old lady, excitedly.

'Yes, and here are the apples. They're so red and juicy and...' Rapunzel started, but did not finish.

'Wonderful!' interrupted the old woman. She whistled, and waited for Rapunzel to start sobbing again. Then, as quick as a flash, she snatched the well-earned apples and replaced them with Jasmine's expensive pearls.

'Pearls?' asked Rapunzel.

'No time to explain. Sorry!' yelled the little old woman, dashing away gleefully from the market.

Rapunzel was angry, but she got over it because she realised that, actually, she'd rather have pearls than apples.

Back at home, the old woman chatted to her cat, telling Puffles all about her wild experiences.

As per usual, Puffles could only meow, and showed no understanding whatsoever. Doris began to gather the ingredients together in preparation for baking a *perfect* pie. She spent hours in the kitchen, for *everything* had to be just right for her guests. She was just about to sit down when the phone rang again. She answered it and Puffles escaped to go outside.

'Hello? Little old woman, cottage number thirty three,' she said.

'Hello, it's me again, the first little piggy. I'm happy to say that we don't need to come to your house anymore; we called Wolf Busters and they cleared our house of the Big Bad Wolf. Then they gave us twenty four pies to eat! Now we won't waste your time and you won't have to cook for us, so that's a weight off your shoulders, isn't it?'

The little old woman slammed the phone down and turned slowly in a rage. 'AAAAARRRRRGGGGHHH,' she screamed.

However, back at the little pigs' house, the Big Bad Wolf was already climbing down the chimney again. He landed in front of the startled pigs, and said, '*Plum pies*? *I'm* not a veggie! I said I like your *plump eyes*, not your plum pies, you silly little piggies...'

...And he blew their house down and chased the pigs all the way to their next home.

IZZY

**Lydia Bossons
(Age 10)**

A fairy with red hair, red wings and a purple dress was going to start flying school tomorrow. Izzy is very shy. She didn't know everyone. So she went to her teacher, Miss Twinkletoes, and she soon had a friend to play with.

She had the nicest girl in the class as her friend. Her friend always said 'Hi' to her and wanted to help her whenever she needed her most.

After a week all of the first years were flying, everyone that was except Izzy - she had to ride a bird.

Tomorrow was the flying performance to everyone. But poor Izzy can't fly, remember! The next day Izzy learnt to fly by flying on her bird to a branch of a tree and jumping off that. On her third try, now with a trampoline below, she jumped and flew round and round in a circle because she could fly!

Even though Izzy was the only person dancing on the ground her mum was still proud of her! After the performance Izzy flew up in the air and did a somersault.

Soon after the show the awards would be called out for the best flying: Award 1- the best in the class, Award 2 - the best in the year and, last but not least, Award 3 - the best in the school.

The award for best in the class went to her friend Ella. The award for best in the year went to Willow and finally the award for best in the school went to - Izzy! Can you believe it!! She actually got best in the school for learning to fly late and doing a somersault of joy.

Izzy's mum was very pleased with her and very proud and now she can say to her friends that her daughter won best in the year at flying. Izzy felt bored with just two friends so she asked some other people to be her friends. Her five new friends were called: Amber, Rose, Matilda, Amy and Lee-Ann. They were very nice and kind friends.

Izzy has finished her life in Year One now. She is moving on to a new year in Year Two...

ANOTHER WORLD

**Hannah Brown
(10 years old)**

Crash! I woke up.

'What was that noise?' I thought. 'And why is it every day when I wake up, I find my toy dolls gathered round my antique tea party set?' It had blue pictures of four leaf clovers. The rest was pale white and it was very delicate. I picked up my pink hair brush and sat on my beautiful stool. I brushed my curly golden hair, got dressed in my pink sparkly dress and brushed my teeth.

'Emily, come down for breakfast!' a voice called. That was my mum. She looked like me. Not only was it that she was like me - that person who always will care about you, someone who will be always nice to you.

'Okay, coming...' I replied. I went down the brown creaky stairs and had my breakfast...

At bedtime, I just had to stay up and find out really what happens. Mum came up to tuck me in my soft feather bed. I pretend to be asleep as she walked out slowly.

'Don't be as slow as a snail!' I said. But I said it in my head.

I stayed up; it felt like forever. An hour maybe. But it was two minutes. I fell asleep in the end. I woke up, I heard voices. There was no time to see the time. I pretended to be asleep. The voices were quiet and squeaky. I tried not to laugh.

'Quiet, you will wake the little girl!' squeaked a voice.

I opened my eyes. There were toys moving round and talking to each other. The toy spotted me and gasped!

'Don't worry. I won't hurt you. Please don't be afraid!' I said calmly, willing them to believe me. I couldn't believe it. They actually believed me.

'Follow me.' said a beautiful doll. So I did. Somehow everything seemed to be growing or was I shrinking? I was shrinking. They went to the teapot, jumped in and disappeared. So what did I do? I jumped in.

There was a world full of toys and Lego houses. It was wonderful.

LIFE or DEATH?

**Tara Prince
Age 13**

Hi, my name is Emily and this is my life. Imagine this. You are walking around when you see a giant serpent that quickly takes pursuit.

I turned and ran. I could hear its heartbeat humming as I went through the forest, trying desperately not to trip. Its hot, sticky breath caught the back of my neck and I only went faster. I knew that, if I fell, it was certain death. They were blood-thirsty killing machines. Not just a few, but millions - taking over the world and destroying the human race. I would be amongst thousands that have already perished. Each one died horrifically, being attacked and then eaten whilst still alive. Sometimes they didn't die until all four limbs had been pulled out with a loud pop. I relived that moment every hour of every day. It happened to my parents, my brother and most of my friends. Only Sophie remained. She wasn't with me now though; she was protecting her family back in the village, just as I did with mine last month. The horror had been going on for six months now and showed no sign of stopping. Then I gasped. And then I fell.

Cautiously, I opened my eyes and sighed in relief. The serpent wasn't there. I was in the local hospital surrounded by nurses.

'How do you feel sweetie?' one asked nicely.

'Fine, why wouldn't I?' I answered and sat up.

Then I remembered. 'Yeah, not too good actually,' I admitted, feeling the long row of stitches along my body. 'Just how badly am I hurt?'

'Well, you lost a lot of blood,' said another nurse.

Then the first one said sadly, 'Someone found you and fought it off. You were almost dead and probably would have been better off that way! We had to revive you three times because the injuries were so bad!'

I winced at the thought of this. Then I thought of Sophie. 'I need to go to the loo,' I said quickly.

They let me go and I snuck out of the window. As I raced towards Sophie's house, I tried to ignore the pain and instead thought of how she might be, alone and without any help.

When I got there, I was all but too late. She lay prostrate on the kitchen floor, lifeless, torn to shreds by one of Them. Tears filled my eyes and I let them flow out. Realizing that all my loved ones were dead, I simply stood motionless, trying to take it in. I thought of its breaking in to her house and grabbing her, her desperate cries of help unheard. Just then I saw a piece of paper on the desk, fluttering in the wind that whistled through the hole in the wall It had made. As I read, I smiled in spite of the situation and made a plan. The note read:

Emily,
I won't make it. I hope you will and defeat It.
GLF is bees.
Good luck!

Your friend,
Sophie x

GLF? I wondered what this meant whilst at the same time, choked up by the message, I left. Then I remembered. Sophie had said that she was trying to find its growth limiting factor.

GLF! I ran into her front room and stared at the fireplace. At that moment, I heard **It** coming. The serpents were breaking down the windows and hurling themselves against the luckily closed door. Momentarily, I dithered in a panic as I considered my actions. But there was no time. They were in. I gritted my teeth and thrust my clenched fist into the bees' nest. I felt a searing hot pain run through my arm as they attacked the intruder. Then I thrust the nest at the quickly approaching serpents and waited. It worked! They began to writhe in pain and throw themselves at the walls. I smiled and started to attack them as well.

Before long they were all gone and the world was safe. Thanks to Sophie.

So that's my story of the end of the world. My scars are only slightly visible now and I am making do with an adopted family. I still miss everyone but that's life I guess.

MY LIFE

Rebekah Marie Taylor
Age 11

My name is Katy, and my life is so not perfect. It used to be, when my parents where together I was happy and fine and had everything I wanted. Then it all changed when my parents split up. I was so upset and even when my dad told me that they were selling the house so mum and dad could split the profits I didn't even care. It was my mum's fault she left dad for some rich skinny twenty seven year old. I lived with dad and hated mum. Little did I know what was going to happen.

'You can't be serious!' I screeched at my dad.

'You have to go and live with your mother in LA for a few weeks or so, sweetheart, she needs to see you as well.' dad mumbled nervously.

'She was the one who left us dad!' I screamed in anger.

'No, Katy.' Dad paused. 'She left *me*,' he sniffed.

'Well, she hasn't bothered to write or call or text me,' I screamed in fury running to my bedroom, sobbing bitterly.

***

Dad drove me to the airport; I guess it was to make sure I actually got on the flight. I didn't look at him the whole drive there, even when he spoke to me I didn't say so much as an "mmm".

When we arrived at Heathrow he said, 'You know I love you Katy, but she is your mum.' Dad sighed.

'I wish she weren't!' I snapped and stormed off, dad traipsing behind me lugging my suitcases behind him. Dad helped me check in. My passport photo is decades old so the lady at the desk squinted hard at me trying to see visualize how a six year old goofy-toothed girl had morphed into a miserable, dark eyed, grumpy teenager.

Finally the lady, faintly smiling said, 'Okay, miss. You're terminal two, gate one; enjoy your flight.'

' 'Bye, sweetheart, love you.' Dad said trying hard to keep back tears. I only said, 'mm'.

***

As I left the passport check desk I spotted a slim blonde haired woman - it was mum!

'Katy! Sweetheart!' She hugged me tightly but I pulled away and stormed off.

'Katy! Katy!' mum said, rushing after me.

She managed to drag me into the cab. Oh, LA was great - the beach, the sights, the boys! But the only dilemma was MUM being all and lovey-dovey (ugh!) with her husband. I slipped away from it all. In my room I opened up my laptop and wrote an email to dad

> *Dear Dad, Hey! Miss you. What's the point in my being here? Mum is just ignoring me! Love, your daughter*
> *Katy*
> *xoxoxox*

I snapped it shut. It was ten o'clock at night so I went to bed. In the morning, mum came up to my room carrying a tray with a glass of orange juice, a chocolate chip muffin and a single pink flower in her best vase.

'Thanks, mum.' I said and hugged her. Suddenly I felt a great surge of relief as I returned the hug and could smell her rosy perfume scent. She held me harder; we held each other close.

From that moment Mum and I were inseparable in LA - shopping, watching a chick flick, at the cinema, eating a meal out and wherever she was, I would be.

***

Mum, dad and I decided to make the visit a normal occurrence. Dad even decided he wanted me to see both parents at the same time over there, so he flew out to LA and bought a flat. Then I started to pick up the pieces of my life. My life was moulding together, but one thing was unresolved - school!

When I entered my new school for the first time I knew I would fit in. There weren't any people who were really cool, just normal people and the occasional brainiac. I soon had four best friends Jenny, Amy, Monica and Rachel.

My life has been completed by one trip! Don't be afraid to take a risk.

INDEX BY TITLE

TITLE	NAME		PAGE

1 Open section

Date Overdue	Mike	Lawrence	71
Dilemma	Bob	Hitching	77
Es ist Heute Einfach Nicht Mein Tag	Charles	Kirkby	81
Five on a Plate	George	Chambers	85
Forever Autumn	Caroline	Hall	27
Giddy-Up, Buttercup	Valerie	Morris	91
Goodbye, Wilf	Bob	Hitching	97
Grapes at Bedtime	Anne	Petersen	101
Greetings to Earth	Tim	Naish	107
Hearts and Poppies	Kathy	Sharp	113
Hit the Road, Jack	S J	Scally	119
Lady in the Red Anorak	Mike	Lawrence	125
Love Songs in Blue Denim	Della	Millward	31
Messing About on the River	Janette	Nourse	129
Mirrors	Diana	Holman	133
Moving On	Jenny	Grant	137
Moving On	Janice	Kirkby-Brown	145
Mr Mean	Bob	Hitching	149
My Holiday	Keith	Hart	33
Never Ending Love Story	Mike	Lawrence	39
Not One of Us	Janice	Kirkby-Brown	45
Noughts and Crosses	Licia	Hitching	153
Our Daily Bread	Janette	Perkins	155
Pretty Flamingo	Tim	Maley	159
Remember Me	Olive	Eastwood	165

Roma Therapy	Mike	Lawrence	**169**
Second Chance	Jenny	Grant	**175**
Seven Days	Clive	Saunders	**181**
Shopping Nightmare	Mike	Lawrence	**185**
Sunshine After the Rain	Moira	Haway	**189**
The Bag of Memories	Shelagh	O'Grady	**195**
The Blue Eyed Boy	Jo	Maycock	**51**
The Choice of a Lifetime	Daniel	Sams	**199**
The Decision	Clare	Connolly	**205**
The Domino Effect	Della	Millward	**211**
The Fare	S J	Scally	**217**
The Ferryman's Wife	Richard	Nicholson	**21**
The Football Match	Ruth	Hughes	**221**
The Hill Top	Jackie	Macintosh	**55**
The Interview	Bob	Hitching	**59**
The Journey	Mary	Coward	**227**
The Riverside Tearooms	Irene	Burnett-Thomas	**231**
The Romance	Bob	Hitching	**237**
Uncomfy	Bob	Hitching	**241**
Walking Back to Happiness	Jenny	Piercy	**245**
Whisky Angel	Sharon	Jones	**65**
Women	Bob	Hitching	**251**

2 Under 18s

Another World	Hannah	Brown	**267**
Izzy	Lydia	Bossons	**263**
Life or Death?	Tara	Prince	**271**
My Life	Rebekah	Taylor	**275**
There's a Wolf in our Oven	Eloise	Orchard	**257**

This book can be obtained by Mail Order

Please send full address details and cheque for £4.99
+ £2.80 for P & P to:

Friends 4 Upton Library, Upton Library, Upton Cross,
Upton, Dorset BH16 5PW

www.F4ul.co.uk

committee@f4ul.co.uk

All profits go to F4UL funds